Tyrant Books
426 West 46th Street Apt. D
NYC 10036

www.NYTyrant.com

Copyright © Annie DeWitt 2016
ISBN 13: 978-0-9913608-4-0
First Edition

Front cover photo Copyright Summer Kellogg / Offset.com
Cover design & author photo by Jerome Jakubiec
resilientandoverwhelmed.com
Interior design by Adam Robinson

WHITE NIGHTS IN SPLIT TOWN CITY

Annie DeWitt

Tyrant Books
New York 2016

I wonder, now, only when it will happen,
when the young mother will hear the
noise like somebody's pressure cooker
down the block, going off. She'll go out into the yard
holding her small daughter in her arms,
and there, above the end of the street, in the
air above the line of trees,
she will see it rising, lifting up
over our horizon, the upper rim of the
gold ball, large as a giant
planet starting to lift up over ours.
She will be standing there in the yard holding her daughter,
looking at it rise and glow and blossom and rise,
and the child will open her arms to it,
it will look so beautiful.

—"When" by Sharon Olds

1.

The car appeared to descend from the sky like the old gray pigeons that skirted the power lines tracing the upheaval of the mountain. Fender, the youngest of the abandoned Steelhead brothers, was sprawled out horizontal over-top of the Jeep, a dare the older boys had put him up to. Maybe he was shackled at the ankles. Maybe he was relying on his own grip. It looked as though his brothers had strapped him there, turned the nose of the 4x4 down the trail, and put the vehicle in neutral. The Jeep had gained enough speed by the time it reached the turnoff onto our little road that its body absorbed any imperfections in the macadam and it surfed over the frost heaves and skids of gravel, catching a bit of warm summer air. Mother stood beside me. We were on our way out to the garden. We stared at the back of Fender's head as it hurtled toward us. The wind took his shirt and its colors billowed up around his face.

Liden, the eldest Steelhead brother, was at the wheel. One of his arms rested across the horn. The other straddled the shoulders of a young girl in a neon tank. The rest of the boys were in the back tending the beer. A long-haired kid tossed cans of Miller High Life out the rear, exploding them over the road. The gold of a can flared in the sunlight before the aluminum burst from the pressure.

This was the summer of 1990. The Berlin Wall fell. The Hubble Space Telescope launched. Mandela was released from prison. Microsoft released a disk, which Father brought home from work, called Windows. Mikhail Gorbachev—The Big Red Splot, my sister Birdie called him—was elected. In school we gathered our pennies to save the whales from Exxon Valdez. Ryan White died of AIDS—"What's AIDS?" Birdie said—"It's a disease of the blood which came from a flight attendant," Mother said over breakfast as Birdie and I discussed the image

1

of the missing girl up the street that plagued the side of our milk cartons. McDonald's had a sign in their window: *Moscow! Shenzhen!* Father read to us from *The Whole Earth Catalog.* Mother framed a photo called "The Pale Blue Dot," which hung over the television. On weekends we watched pirated VHS copies of *The Big Chill.* When Mother turned up the radio real loud and sang "I Heard It Through the Grapevine," I wondered what the grapevine was and what it was they had heard through it. The night Billy Crystal announced *Dances With Wolves* beat out *Ghost* for Best Picture, Father said the whole world had gone soft. "That's your Dad's girlfriend," Mom said to Birdie and I, pointing at Demi Moore on the screen. "I love that you get cold when it's 71 degrees out," Dad said, dramatically, taking Mother in his arms and reenacting his favorite scene from *When Harry Met Sally.* "I came here tonight because when you realize you want to spend the rest of your life with somebody, you want the rest of your life to start as soon as possible."

"Look around you," Mother said, motioning to Birdie and I and the house in the background. "It already started."

At night, Birdie and I ate Hungry Man dinners from TV trays in the Lazy Boy and watched reruns of *I Love Lucy* and *Dick Van Dyke.* The future, as I saw it, was predicted by the likes of Jane Jetson and Hulk Hogan. In twenty years we would all be wearing beehives and driving hovercrafts while R2-D2 floated around the kitchen cooking us the morning's oats. Operation Desert Storm blasted in the background while stay-at-home mothers drove their Honda Accords around newly minted cul-de-sacs on the other side of town. Farmers sold off old Indian burial grounds while listening to Billy Joel's "We Didn't Start the Fire" and Janet Jackson's "Rhythm Nation." Every night the man on the news said, "It's ten o'clock, do you know where your children are?" and Father would laugh, "No. Do you?"

For me, the image of Fender Steelhead sprawled out kite-like tethered to the rack of the Jeep was the beginning of some deeper treason. I had never wanted to rescue something in such earnest. I had the feeling this was the moment in life I'd heard Uncle talk about, the one in which fate comes to a halt in the middle of the road in front of you. In such a moment you were outside of your body watching yourself step over a thin white line that represented a wide unforgiving chasm, but in reality looked so small an inkling you almost mistook it for some fissure the wind had drawn in the sand.

I'd buried a hamster once in a box in the yard. It had cracked its leg on the little wheel in its cage and was only half-dead when I found it, hanging mid-flight on its circuit. Uncle put it out on the porch in a small yellow shoebox to finish dying. Every few hours, he went out and shook the box. It took the whole afternoon before there was no more shake in the body. We buried the box off the end of the cement stoop that lined the front of the house. I didn't know how long it took for an animal to suffocate. Even as we covered the box with dirt, I wasn't so sure it wasn't still gasping a little at its own air.

"It's not like you can just snap the neck," Uncle had said.

There wasn't a soul alive or dead that cared whether Fender Steelhead kept his heels on the ground or went flying. For Fender, to fit was the whole of it. He needed to find someway into his brothers' breed. If it wasn't the wrestling or the smut or the holes in the wall, it was the flying. The getting pissed and high. The letting go. From the moment I saw him barreling toward me, I knew it would be hard. It would be bitter. There would be that New England fence between us, our feet planted firmly on opposite sides.

The problem was, Fender had already usurped my own cutting loose.

"It's a shame too," Mother said of the boys as the Jeep turned the corner.

I stared at the back of Fender's shirt as the Wrangler sped out of sight.

"You don't look at people like that," Mother laughed, cuffing me gently on the back of the head. It was a phrase she often repeated, though I didn't yet know its importance.

"You don't look at people like that," Mother said later that summer.

I recognized the phrase but by then I had lost the memory of its earlier context and felt only the tender surge of familiarity that Mother's advices sometimes lent.

"Like what?" I said.

"The way you were looking at him. It's not done at your age. It's unsightly."

We were sitting at the table overlooking the window in Otto Houser's kitchen. Otto had invited Mother, Birdie, and I over for lunch. Father was at work. Granny Olga was down for her nap. Otto wanted to extend his hand back toward Mother's trust.

"Don't touch anything," Mother had said to Birdie and I on our way over to Otto's. "I'm not saying it's their fault. They're old is all. All they have is their germs."

"It doesn't spread like that," I said.

"What doesn't spread like what," Mother said.

"What she has," I said.

"What *who* has," Mother repeated.

"His Helene," I said. "Otto says she been sick so long whatever she's down with is too worn out to jump anywhere else."

Birdie leapt a little then in the road. She liked to try out the tricks they were teaching all the gymnasts at the gym. Small and round and tow-headed, Mother said Birdie was the type of child who would show up well on television. The nickname had stuck despite Father's better efforts. He thought perhaps Birdie would be blind to her own charm and good looks. He'd wanted to see his youngest fashioned with a name with history behind it. "Don't turn her into a bore," Mother had said. "She's got such a thrust for life."

"It's my new tumble," Birdie said that morning, cartwheeling in the road.

"Very good, darling," Mother said. "That was *very* good."

Even still, Mother insisted we wash Otto Houser's clean silver before we set the table. She'd seen that boy Ryan White on the television. There was a cancer afoot in Otto's house and she wasn't going to catch it, worn out or not. Otto was at the other end of the counter whipping the mayo and mashing the tuna. Mother took the spoons out of the drawer right in front of the old man's face and washed them again. She heard the whisk of his fork stop against the side of the bowl.

"You must have been quite lucky once," Mother said.

"How do you figure?" Otto said, glancing at Mother from the corner of his eye as he went to cut another can of fish on the opener under the cabinet.

"Your wife kept quite a kitchen," Mother said nodding toward the living room where His Helene was asleep on the couch. "Everything at arms length. You can tell it's just how Helene left it."

We started laughing then. Me and the old man. Me and Otto Houser. Me and the Otto that was still hanging on that banister somewhere waiting for his wife and his tap lesson.

"You two have been spending some time together in my absence," Mother said. "You and my daughter have adopted the same laugh."

This made Otto howl even harder. Wilson was in on it then. He wanted to prove that he spoke his old man's language. Wilson was full-grown with graying hair that was balding in the back. People said he was slow. Mother said he'd been touched by something. When he spoke, flecks of spittle formed around his mouth so that, if you were made to stand too close to him, you'd feel a fine mist. He lived in the RV out back. The trailer was parked on the lawn close to the porch. When Otto propped open the door, he could sit on his crumbling veranda and keep watch over his aging son.

That summer Wilson had started gumming a toothpick. Whenever you talked to him, he often repeated whatever you'd said, like he'd gotten stuck on a word and couldn't get past it. In his confusion, the toothpick dropped out of the corner of his mouth and into the dirt. Without pause, Wilson picked it up off the ground and righted it back between his lips.

"Beg your pardon," Otto Houser said to Mother when he'd come down a little. "It's just been so damn sad around here. You can't imagine."

"I can imagine a lot of things," Mother said.

She turned then to Wilson.

"Your laugh is infectious," she said. She looked at him, taking his chin in her hand and examining both sides of his face.

"Infectious," Wilson said.

"It means you give people something," Mother said. "You give them something happy." She clasped Wilson's cheeks momentarily and kissed him on the lips. The kiss appeared almost an accident, a way for Mother to direct her focus toward something other than Otto's laughter.

Wilson's body shot up from his chair from the excitement.

"Infectious," he chanted under his breath, going over the word with his mouth until he could form it properly. After a while the chanting got louder until he was yelling. There was something garish about watching a big man flail about indoors. Despite his hunch, Wilson cut a good six-foot and a half. His head almost touched the ceiling fan. The house was old. The ceilings were low.

Wilson kept on until no one was laughing. Otto looked like he'd had the wind taken out of him. The lines in his face deepened. He curled his lips and ran them over the length of his teeth. Otto took great care of himself and his things to be sure they never disappointed him. There was something about poverty of any kind, emotional or otherwise, which he found unsettling.

"I'm sorry," Mother said after a minute. "I didn't mean to start anything."

"No harm done," Otto said. "Sometimes my son stumbles on something new and can't get past it."

"Well," Mother said. "That's a blessing isn't it. Most days I would kill to find something new to amuse me. One could *live* for that kind of excitement."

"That depends," Otto said. "On how much newness you can stand witnessing in a man his age."

"I think he's charmed," Mother said. "I find him refreshing."

No one spoke for a minute. I had never known anyone to put Otto so much into his place. Even Wilson sensed the tension and settled back down in his chair.

"Go on, Son," Otto said to him. "Like the lady says, dance wherever you damn well please. Burn the house down."

There wasn't much room at Otto's kitchen table. We all crowded in. Wilson took up nearly two chairs, all his weight settled under the belt. Otto took Birdie on his knee to compensate. Birdie picked at his plate. She didn't much care for crust or fish. The tuna was thick and moist. There was so much to say between the whole of us, nobody could get any of it out.

Otto stared out the bay window that looked out over the pasture. After a while, he started talking about a dream he'd had several days previous about an indigenous community that had resurrected a series of tenement houses on stilts to allow the water to pass underneath. The people carried their belongings around on their backs during the day in case their houses were missing when they returned home from fishing. The houses, called kelongs, were built without nails, depending on rattan to bind the tree trunks and boards. Otto had read about it once in a back issue of *National Geographic* his wife had left behind years ago on his desk in the barn.

"Kelongs," Otto Hauser said that afternoon, squaring his fingers in front of his mouth and blowing underneath them like a river rushing forward. The movement of his breath tousled my bangs across the table.

I heard keys turning in the entryway door. The light in the front hall flicked on casting an odd glare over the living room where His Helene was asleep. I wondered who had stopped in on us and sat back, easy-like, in my chair. Otto Hauser seemed oblivious to the sound of the keys or the quality of the light that day. Looking across the table at the old man holding up his diorama of this invisible house, I pictured the Steelhead brothers' Jeep tumbling full-speed down the hill earlier that summer looking as though it just might crash into the doorway of the Bottom Feeder where Mother and I had stood watching.

As the car descended the mountain, Mother had shifted her weight to her outside foot, leaning her hip against the interior wood of the doorframe so the structure could support her recline. I had stood silently next to her, encased in the rectangular entryway of our home. Together, I had thought, our postures alone might hold the house up.

"I just hope they've got some good brakes on that thing," Mother had said looking up at Fender Steelhead patterning against the sky like some great gull. "I hope they plan on using them."

2.

The hill on our front lawn housed what Father called two trees of knowledge, old apple trees that flowered in the spring and shed small bitter apples in the fall. The yearly continuation of this cycle was inexplicable. Having fallen under the care of a long line of neglectful owners who had failed to prune away the dead wood to make way for the new sprouts, their fruit all but went to seed on the branch. And yet each spring the trees sprouted great plumage, large white blossoms that, if you sat at the base of the trees, smelled like a mixture of honey and vinegar.

I attributed this cycle to what I'd once heard Mother call the wayside of things. "The wayside of what?" I'd said. Mother was sitting in the living room then, in her blue bathrobe, her arm draped over the couch near the back window which she had cracked just wide enough that she could ash out of it.

"The wayside of life," she said. She tapped her cigarette on the sill and stared vacantly across the deck, her eyes trained on the three men on horseback who were cresting the top of Fay Mountain, about to disappear under the power lines that ran down the back.

Mother extinguished her cigarette, flicking the butt out the window. She got up to turn on the fan so that the smoke blew out over the porch and the air came back into the room. As she sat back down on the couch, she leaned slightly forward and folded her hands. This position was the way she introduced speaking opportunities, times when she would tell me something I wasn't supposed to hear. Times I would listen. The thing I learned from this opportunity was that the wayside was a place where Father had brought her, this house on a road with aging neighbors where a city girl like herself lost the occasion to put on a pair of decent shoes and escape the house.

Mother had a whole closet of shoes. They were lined up on the floor in the back under her dresses. Birdie and I tried them on evenings when she and Father went out. We were always careful to put them back just in their order. We called these shoes her lady slippers. We had first heard about the extraordinary nature of lady slippers when Father pointed them out to us one afternoon while hiking the land out back of the house. The flowers were rare. They were small and white and delicate, like the inside of a child's palm planted in the grass.

Being that we grew up on the wayside, Birdie and I often burned off the afternoon hunting about the yard, inventing games under the trees. These games were best played when the grass had just been mowed and the clippings stuck to your body. Afterward, when you got a good hosing, you could really see the grass coming down, you could really watch yourself being stripped of earth.

From his window across the street, Otto Houser watched our games of rolling down the hill and blasting each other with the hose. He said it looked like we were wearing our birthday suits. But, there weren't any birthdays that summer. Birdie was born in May. I was born in November.

In the evenings, Otto sat on the couch in front of his picture window and watched me finger away at the piano. The learning books came in a box with a set of tapes, which I listened to each day before sitting down and reading the notes. The piano was an old baby grand, an antique Father had bought at the town hall flea market from the cabinetmaker who sold restored furniture out of his flatbed. The only room large enough for Baby was the portico at the front of our house where Mother kept the dining table her parents had sent her, the one with the feet that looked like bird talons. Father called the table Old Eagle Back.

The morning Baby arrived, Father moved Old Eagle Back into the basement. Mother was at church. The man who delivered Baby was there to help.

"All a man needs, Jean," Father told me as he carried Old Eagle across the living room and down the stairs. "A little bit of music. And an extra set of hands."

Baby was an instant hotshot. All black around the body, she came with a hood that you propped open when you played to let the music out. Sometimes after practice, I'd imagine crawling under the hood and closing the top over me, just to feel the tension in the strings.

For a short stint after Baby arrived Father's brother joined us over a series of weekends. Uncle's real name was Dutch but everyone called him Sterling. Sterling lived a few hours away in a small manufacturing city. He worked at a plastics factory and lived in an old two-story motel where he kept a permanent room. What I knew of Uncle was that he had a strong alto voice and a red sports car. Those nights he joined us, Father drank cans of light beer while Sterling told stories about the men who worked next to him at the plastics factory over bottles of wine and fingers of Old Granddad. Sterling got on too much about old times.

"Leave it alone," Father'd say.

"Is it wrong for a man to talk about his father?" Sterling would say, and they'd retire to the piano.

Sterling had a penchant for Italian opera. It was one of many tastes no one could account for. Those nights he visited, Sterling sang at Father's back, performing long stretches of lively arias with precision and grace, defying any suggestion of handicap by the hour or the bottle.

Why he dropped in on us that short stint of nights that summer, Father couldn't explain. Several weeks after his arrival, Sterling took his red sports car and drove west toward the desert for several days until he reached the part of the country where the grass gets tall and his little red car could disappear among the sheaves of wheat like an ant navigating through thick blades of crab grass. This was how I pictured that part of the country and the distance it put between me and Uncle in my mind. "Big Sky

Country," Sterling had once described it. "Out there you get a piece of sky bigger than the view from New Guinea. All you got to do is step outside and you feel like you could pull a bird down from the clouds with your own two hands. That's how close you are to your own expectations. You don't have to go climbing any mountains just to feel so small and alive. Just walking the fields you start to feel your arms lift a little."

Father abandoned the piano for several weeks after Sterling left. It sat empty for a string of evenings until one night after dinner, I took up again with my method. I was determined to will some part of Sterling's freedom back into our lives before it abandoned us entirely.

Thus, I first came to notice Otto Houser during a period of great mourning. Our introduction came as I got up to open the window one evening after practice. The heat that night was thick. It was as though the radiator had been bled for the first time that season and a hot steam had descended over our little road. Under the lamp, my face was slick with sweat. My body was dank and my bathing suit clung to my crotch. I stood at the window hoping to catch some movement in the air.

Otto was sitting on his porch, not unusual given the hour. In my experience, the heat often drove people outdoors. Being that I was young, I was still under the guise that I was shielded by darkness. I could barely make out the outline of the old man's figure in the gathering darkness of the veranda. I stared at him for a moment while picking at my swimsuit and wiping the sweat from my brow.

This particular bathing suit had allure. The allure was the reason I had chosen it, had barely taken it off my body since I had picked it off the rack. It was white with three holes on each side, which were fastened together with pink plastic buttons. When I lifted my arms toward the piano, you could see three patches of flesh running up the side of my body. This, I imagined, was what people meant by "untouchable combinations." I'd heard a neighbor use those words once when telling Father an anecdote about breeding. He'd recently sired a Doberman with a Golden

12

Retriever. "In the end," he said, "You're looking at a good, kind dog with a strong snout. The snout gives the Doberman away, but it's the combination that's untouchable." This was also how I imagined Sterling's actress friend would have dressed for him.

When I played, Otto Houser said he had the feeling that he was glimpsing some rare, unidentified talent. He observed me from across the road. The details of the piece, he said, he could not discern at his precise distance. From his place on the porch, unable to hear the sounds I made, he watched instead for some forward thrust in my body to suggest the recurrence of a chord or the emergence of melody. He particularly admired those passages where the thin waft of one of my arms eagled-out as it ran up and down an octave. Otto enjoyed those segments of the old television variety hours that featured some new emerging talent, often a corn-fed, blond-haired youth with his or her sights set on the big city lights. These displays of talent produced a rising in Otto's chest, he said. Their fame nearly embraced him.

On the warmer days, I played in the mornings before the sun was already on us. One noon after practice I went out into the yard to get the mail. Otto Houser was sitting in a rusty beach chair he'd brought onto his porch. Later, once I'd come to know him, he said when the sun was overhead and the shade was right, he liked to sit under the cover of the veranda and eat peanuts while he watched me play. He liked to suck the salt off the shells.

"Hey, Hotshot," Otto called across the road to me the first afternoon we spoke. I turned to look at him. It was the first time I had known a man to notice me. I could see my reflection in the window at his back. There wasn't much curve to me. Twelve going on thirteen, I'd grown four inches that year. My chest was still flat. I hadn't yet embodied the weight of the world, as Mother said. I fumbled with the mail. One of the envelopes slipped off the top of the stack.

"You missed a note," Otto said.

3.

Early that summer, Mother took a vision of England under her wing. She fell in with Margaret Nydam, the elderly British widow who lived in the studio apartment above the Agway in the center of town. Margaret was Fay Mountain's only living European transplant. Along with her accent and her collection of Yeats, Margaret boasted purebred old world blood. The Women's Voting League congregated in her parlor every Sunday where Margaret served scones and cream. Father often called Margaret cultural driftwood. Her influence, he said, floated wherever it was least needed. She was also the town librarian.

Most mornings that summer I awoke to Margaret sitting on the wooden stool next to our kitchen counter where Mother sat when she sorted the bills. Margaret sipped a black coffee. Mother would put out a spread until Margaret chided her enough that she'd finally retire to the table with her cigarette and tea. Mother was constantly extending the life of her teabag with fresh water until the brew was so weak it tasted like a river of stirred up silt. "One of anything goes a long way," she said.

Margaret arrived in the early hours cloaked in layers of felt and flannel and an old safety pin where she'd thrown up her bangs. Layers, Margaret said, trapped the breeze. A husky body odor emanated from the places where Margaret exposed her pallor to the light. Due to her age and thickness of her hair, the oils made her face glow and gave her hair body. Her long unkempt grays were braided to one side her face. Margaret was not in the habit of wearing undergarments. I had glimpsed her breasts once where they hung away from her skin as she bent over to adjust her stool and pour herself another trifle from her flask. The immodesty of my gaze seemed to impress her.

That morning, the two women were hanging a painting in the kitchen above Old Eagle Back. Margaret sat on the stool observing Mother work.

"What about here," Mother said, holding the painting at shoulder level against the far wall of the kitchen. "How's that for height?"

"That's fine," Margaret said. "That's just fine. Mark it off. I've got a level in back of the car. I'll make a dash for it after we finish our tea."

Mother took the pencil from behind her ear and drew a faint line on the wall over the center of the frame.

The wall had been a focal point of Mother's recent discomfort. It sat at the far end of the house onto which both the living room and the portico overlooked. The previous owners of the house had been an elderly couple with a fondness for stenciling pastoral scenes onto any stretch of wall that enjoyed some open expanse. To Mother's mind, the kitchen offered a particularly unforgivable example. The laymen's handiwork, she felt, was evidence of the house's age and limited possibility.

"Like Didion said," Margaret said. "Style is character."

"Truly," Mother said. She leaned the print against the wall and stood back to regard it as she smoked.

In truth, I could tell Mother wasn't entirely sure about the choice of the work. The print had been a gift from Margaret, an old replica from her wall, which Margaret said she'd stared at too long.

"It needs fresh eyes," Margaret had said, putting the frame into the back of her Volvo one night after the two women had gotten into the sherry.

Mother looked disappointed now with her choice. She'd hoped for something more modern. In the wake of their enthusiasm, she'd ended up with Georgia O'Keeffe's "Red Hills."

"There's a hardness about it," Margaret said. "It radiates a certain intelligence."

Mother searched the soft red expanse of the print for the intelligence of which Margaret spoke. In her worst imaginings, I thought, the earthen mass looked not unlike one of the watercolors Birdie would bring home from school. At best, it radiated a kind of optimism.

"It's a horizon," Mother said.

"Not only that," Margaret said. "It's Texas."

"Really," Mother said.

"Truly," Margaret said. "O'Keeffe attended art school in Chicago. The boys there were always encouraging her to abandon her practice and become an art teacher or a live model. One even went so far as to paint over her work to show her how the Impressionists made trees. At twenty-four, O'Keeffe said she moved to Texas because there were no trees to paint."

"In that case I understand her prerogative," Mother laughed dragging long and hard on her cigarette before pushing the smoke out her nose.

"When they got too bored of looking at the horizon," Margaret said. "O'Keeffe and her sister, Claudia, used to go out and trace the evening stars. They'd take long walks and Claudia would play skeet with the bottles in the road, throwing the bottles up into the air and picking off as many of them as she could before they hit the ground."

"Don't tempt me," Mother laughed.

"You're a funny woman, Ania," Margaret said to Mother. "In fact, you're not so unlike Didion yourself."

"Come off it," Mother said by way of encouragement.

"Scout's honor," Margaret said. "When the men asked her why she painted 'Red Hills' instead of her traditional flowers, O'Keeffe replied, 'A red hill doesn't touch anyone's heart.'"

Mother wasn't much versed in the ways of Didion. She associated writers of that ilk with the allure she had felt towards the women's movement that had erupted during her college years. The product of Russian immigrants who had raised their family in a small boarding house in one of New York's smaller industrial cities, she had avoided her attraction to the movement for practicality's sake. Her mindset was the product of the immigrant constitution. She'd been taught to keep her brow tipped slightly toward the heavens at all times such that her very posture might raise her up. While her grade school friends were tattooing their books with pictures of Kennedy, she'd attended Republican meetings with her father at the General Electric. The first vote she'd cast had been for Nixon. From a young age she'd wanted to be a part of the American politic, a forecast she associated with the Republican brain. Republicans belonged to a set of wealthy risk-takers with strong characters who made good on their children and their investments. "The future is portended in the rise of one's cheekbones," Mother often said. "That slender slope." Mother had spent one summer of her college career working desk duty at the addictions division of the Red Cross, conducting intake interviews with the Veterans. She'd felt she'd seen enough that summer to know big government didn't accomplish anything more than organizing people's worst years.

Mother now spent what evenings she could out of the house. She took night classes that met at the feed store in the center of town. The nights she wasn't studying, she attended meetings held by The League of Women Voters in Margaret's studio. Beyond voting, the league was dedicated to promoting speaking opportunities. Mother had begun exercising these around the house with Birdie and I.

Despite her conservative politic, Mother was fiercely imaginative and outspoken, attributes ignited by those Sunday sit-ins. Margaret appreciated Mother's thrift and her libel. She recognized in the young woman a similar passion for bargaining with the world. Despite the gap in their age and their experience, life had lent both women the perspective that the only interesting lives were those lived by people whose subsistence required very little upkeep, yet whose true thriving was provided for by acts of excess. Margaret smoked and threw dinner parties. Socially Mother cavorted with the town's few peaked progressives. She danced in the kitchen to Elvis. Margaret brought some color back into her cheeks.

"I'm just not sure this print's particularly modern," Mother said that morning, regarding the O'Keeffe where it rested against our kitchen wall.

"Look around you," Margaret chided, "Next to that window, the painting almost looks like a mirror image of your little view."

"So now you're saying I've bought a house with a dismal view," Mother laughed.

"Precisely," Margaret laughed.

"It's depressing," Mother said. "Staring at all that red in the distance. It's like someone rained blood on the mountain."

"Color overthrows form," Margaret said. "Really, it's a very *modern* idea."

As if to lend credit to her heritage, Margaret was a gifted photographer. Her husband had worked for the Audubon Society and was rumored to have been a distinguished botanist and nature writer. In an act of affection for him, Margaret had taken up photography and had often accompanied him on his trips. Mr. Nydam had died some years before Margaret came to own her apartment above the Agway—really more of an attic studio than home—which now housed her plethora of nature books, hardcover photography manuals, and a collection of photographic equipment that harked back to another era. One volume documented the mission of an environmental photographer to chart the Earth's topography, a solitary job performed under some level of duress and extremity of climate. Along with several scrapbooks of newspaper clippings and an indexed library of field guides, the manuals, cameras, and other photographic equipment made up the entirety of the existing relics of Margaret's husband's fabled career. I imagined Mr. Nydam, writer, philanthropist, bird enthusiast, disappearing from society for several days at a time, knee-deep in swamplands, charting the growth of exotic flora and fauna while predicting local weather trends based on the migratory patterns of various flocks of sandpiper and wood thrush.

The Nydams never had any children. Margaret was a woman with whom other women could relinquish all memories of childbirth and breast-feeding. She unbuckled herself after dinner and enjoyed a glass of good sherry with the occasional fag. This idea, or some combination thereof, made Mother giddy. She came home from those Sunday evenings at Margaret's smelling faintly of smoke and brandy, some new book or broach that Margaret had lent her tucked away in her purse.

Father called the group The Separatists.

"Where you going, Rick?" Mother would say those evenings after supper when Father pulled a cigar from his pocket and lit off up the road toward the butte which overlooked the highway.

"A lady needs time for leisure," Father would say.

I knew Father kept a box of White Owls in the glove compartment of his Bronco. The cigars were individually wrapped and sealed with thin strips of paper on which was displayed the white bird perched on his branch. Below the bird the emblem read: New Yorker, Est. 1887. I'd taken to stealing the tossed wrappers from the backseat of Father's car.

Those nights Father went out walking, I imagined he found himself looking up at the familial scenes which presented themselves in the windows of the neighboring houses on Fay Mountain. Perhaps he was impressed with the scale of life they presented. The most important goal in life was to author something authentic, he'd tell us. There was something handsome in it. He'd insisted we call him Pop. Father was what he had called his old man. It had too much of the dictator in it, he said.

"So you're saying O'Keeffe had a certain artificial intelligence," Mother said that morning.

"I'm saying she had a certain hardness, is all," Margaret said.

I regarded the print from where I stood in the kitchen. To me, it looked like a reflection of Mother herself, bold and red and sprawling.

Content with their handiwork, Margaret surrendered to the news. Since the war had started, Mother had kept a small television on the counter so we could follow the headlines.

"I'll never get used to it," Mother said.

"Used to what?" Margaret said.

"The continuity of all this coverage. I keep thinking they've dropped a bomb over there every time my teacups rattle a little in my kitchen. I find myself pacing the house waiting for the sirens to sound."

"You're a product of your generation," Margaret said.

"I'm a product of the space race," Mother said. "Growing up, I remember looking out the window one winter and thinking the Russian's had finally bombed us. It turns out it was just the first snow."

"What sirens?" I said.

"The air raids, baby," Mother said. "I went to school during the Cold War. Several days a week we had a drill. An alarm would sound and we'd hide under our desks."

"What were you protecting yourself against," I said.

"A big red scream, darling," Margaret said.

"Never mind all that, baby," Mother said. "Come here and watch the news."

I tried to imagine what a cold war would look like. I pictured a tundra of ice with soldiers frozen into it. To my mind, the current war in the desert was humorless. The endless shots of the soldiers which plastered the screen at all hours of the day lacked temperature or color. Those evenings Father returned late from work, Birdie, Mother and I ate TV dinners on folding trays in the living room. Mother liked to listen to Brokaw. She watched interviews with the POW's in silent anticipation. I had recently come upon Mother standing in front of her bathroom mirror one morning imagining that she herself was participating in the coverage. An old college flame of hers had once been a filmmaker. He'd written one screenplay — *Did I Wake You Up?* For a brief stint in the seventies under his tutelage, Mother had entertained the idea of becoming a newscaster. She and her flame would sit up nights and he would interview her about her reactions to life at her women's college, which was considering becoming Co-ed.

"What do you make of America's response to this new war as a child of the Vietnam generation," I had seen Mother ask herself into the old wooden handle of her hairbrush.

"It has a certain hardness about it," Mother had replied.

There was, Mother taught me, a certain liberty in reflecting upon the experiences of one's previous lives.

The news that morning with Margaret and the O'Keeffe was interrupted by a knock at the front door.

"Sorry to interrupt on a weekend, Ma'am," the Ranger standing on our porch said. "Is your husband at home?"

"I'm sure he is," Mother replied studying him through the gaps in the screen. "May I ask who's inquiring?"

"I drove up from town," the Ranger said, removing his hat so you could see the contours of his face where the sun hit them. "I'm here to inquire about your stream. We've had complaints about the pests in these parts."

Two large, clear gullys of sweat ran down the side of his face. His hair was wet where the hat had been. A uniform often makes a man look older than he is, I thought. To a man of his age, pest was a specimen of experience no larger than biology.

Father must have heard the whine of the screen door. He emerged from the bulkhead where he'd been sorting packets of seeds. A long-winded pride swelled from Father's chest as he watched the Ranger interacting with Mother. Mother had a way of casting men outside of themselves. It was in such moments that Father was most dumbfounded by his own good luck.

"I can see you located my trouble here, Ranger," Father called to us, curling the thick, green hose around the underbelly of his arm.

"No trouble," The Ranger said. "I just came to inquire about having a look around your stream."

"Is there some issue with my stream?" Father said.

"Well, that depends, I suppose," the Ranger said stepping off the porch and heading toward the bulkhead where Father was wrapping his hose. "On what you call trouble. There's been talk of dredging your stream to rid the town of the squeeters and the gnats. A doctor recently built a home on the east side of the mountain. A city man. High-up on his profession. With all the horse farms in these parts, there's been rumor of equine encephalitis. The doctor's wife is pregnant."

The road was thick with bugs that summer. Inside the house, Mother had taken to hanging flytraps in the doorways. The thin, sticky yellow papers hung from the doorframes like rows of gristle. When the breeze came through the windows at night, it shook the papers, unsticking the carcasses that were less deeply embedded and unleashing them onto the ground. In the morning, the linoleum under the doorframe which led to the kitchen was littered with small wings and dried up bodies which Mother swept into the dustpan and threw out over the deck. She said the protein was good for her garden. Every now and again she missed a spot and you felt the crunch of a dried fly underfoot.

Above all things, Father prided himself on reason and what levelheadedness he could offer others less informed about the world than himself. Since moving to Fay Mountain, Birdie and I had been bitten by horseflies big enough to stop a cockroach in it's tracks. Father knew that doctor's baby was at no immediate risk. If he had been a betting man, he'd have put money on it. Talk, Father often said, had a reliable pattern. Most of the gossip which made its way to Fay Mountain Road had nearly extinguished itself in town before it reached us. Father took the Ranger out back of the house to the marshland where the stream emptied out just to appease him. Dressed in my bathing suit and Mother's gardening boots, I accompanied the two men to determine what opportunity might lie dormant in the air.

The heat that day was dry and unsettling. The sun was strong and blocked out all sense of movement. Even the mosquitoes in the swamp seemed to have settled down under the leaves of the trees to find a moist spot in the shade and avoid choking on the dust. The stream coughed out a trickle. The marsh itself looked like a bald piece of earth, dry and cracked in some patches, wet enough in others that the land moved like jelly underfoot. We made our way—the Ranger, Father and I—down to the tributary where the stream emptied out into a small basin. At the mouth of the basin, a beaver had built a den out of twigs and torn bits of burlap, remnants of old feedbags that had been carried down-stream from the pastures in the runoff. A green plastic soda bot-tle had caught on the south face of the den and bobbed listlessly in the water. As we crossed the dam, Father picked up the bottle and stuffed it in his pocket while I made my way toward the left bank of the stream to get a better view of the marsh. There, we surveyed the land for clouds of bugs. "You know those well-to-do folk," the Ranger said by way of apology. "Always looking for someplace to cast around their improvement. They'd mow their neighbor's lawn if it would make their own look greener."

The left bank of the river sat slightly higher than the marsh-land below it. Amid the floating lily pods and clusters of cat-o'-nine-tails, it resembled an island around which the earth dropped off. An old white birch stood alone in the center of the island. The tree no longer bore leaves. Instead, it boasted a full head of barren branches whose thin, paper-like bark resembled the skin of a cabbage, nearly transparent in the morning sun.

"Finders keepers," Father said as he made his way up the bank. Beneath the tree, he hoisted me up by the waist and set me on one of the lower branches.

"Hold on to this," Father said, handing me the bottle out of his pocket. "If you want to claim a place for your own, you've got to learn to tend your land. The Ranger and I are just going to take a quick swing around back of the marsh to see if we can rustle ourselves up some of those baby killers," he laughed. "Won't go far enough to let you out of eyesight. You keep a look out, yah hear?"

The two men turned and started for the far end of the marsh.

"Now that's what I call a little piece of gold," I heard the Ranger say before they disappeared from earshot. The Ranger tipped his hat in my direction as the two men picked their way across the swamp.

When they had vanished into specks on the other side of the marsh, I slid out of the tree and made my way to the left bank of the river. Seated there, I put the empty bottle to my lips and blew over top of it. Sometimes at night when Father was at the piano, Mother sang a song about going to San Francisco. They called this song their old standard. I tried to remember the tune but nothing came except the sound of air rushing over the hollow glass like the whistle of a train as it grew near.

4.

With the scare on, people kept their horses in the barn most days despite the weather. Otto Houser said this was rubbish. In ten years, he claimed, the whole country had only seen the loss of a few good animals. Fewer bodies, he said, than he could count on one hand. Sleeping sickness, as it was known by the farmers, was a disease that affected the greenhorns, those people who lived backwater and liked to keep a filly or two cooped up in a barbwire paddock so small the horses stood in their own manure and ate whatever shrubs made their way up through the filth onto dry land.

But when word reached the feed store that a Palomino had fallen sick two counties over, even Otto Houser took to keeping his horses in the barn from before dusk to well after sunup, those hours when the mosquitoes were at their peak. Otto claimed he did it to protect the boarders he stabled at the barn. His own, he said, could fare. After a while, even the old all-weather Shetland Otto kept out of doors and rotated around the various paddocks to graze down the weeds and eat back the scrub brush had disappeared from the field and into the barn. Most mornings, we woke to the sound of horses kicking the insides of their stalls.

When Birdie and I pedaled our bikes over the bridge to the farm stand, we saw Cash at work in the fields, the thin outline of his body hunched over in the cab of the bright orange baler as it worked its way across the earth, dividing the grassy spoils into neat rows of hay that cut across the west side of the mountain.

Fender manned the register at the farm stand while Ada sat in the shade of the overhang in front of the old garage within shouting distance of the customers. Just short of four feet and built like a lumberjack, Ada had a shock of red hair that ran down her back in a long braid. She spoke to her customers like they were inviting in the type of trouble she'd worked all her life to keep out. Women liked her because she could be trusted around their husbands. Men liked her because she could jump-start a car on a hill without cables in a pinch. The meaner Ada was to you, the higher you ranked in her opinion.

In winters, Ada went stir crazy. Without the constant drone of customers to meddle with, she took to the offensive, canning enough leftover produce to feed an army of squatters. The local newspaper ran a feature about it. Ada stacked the cans in the old carriage shed that had once housed their vehicles and farm equipment. Forced to keep his equipment out in the open, the joke went that after a snowfall Cash had to shovel out his own plow. If you drove by their property in winter, you could make out the faint outline of a backhoe towering over the empty corn-field gathering snow.

That summer, Ada had turned an old wooden carriage on end so the wheel made a table. Ada sat behind this table most after-noons in a rusted-out folding chair, playing checkers with Wil-son. It seemed the two hardly moved position.

As Birdie and I turned our bikes into the gravel driveway one afternoon after the Ranger's visit, Wilson got up from his chair. He began undoing his belt and moving his hips back and forth in the air.

"Stop saluting those girls," Ada said, reaching into her apron for a folded up newspaper and cuffing him on the bald spot on the back of his head.

Wilson pumped his hips so hard the air moved, and for the first time that summer, I could feel a slight breeze take the hairs at the base of my neck.

"You stay put with the bikes," I said to Birdie. Birdie was afraid of Wilson. She didn't understand why an old man was interested in a couple of kids. Otto's faded blue Cadillac turned into the drive.

The car was as wide as the road and moved like a boat. Dust kicked up around it and the sun cast a glare on the windshield, behind which I could make out two well-tanned shoulders in the front seat. A woman climbed out of the car, swinging her legs out from under the dash where they had been resting in Otto's lap.

"Afternoon, Ada," Otto said.

"Afternoon, Otto," Ada said without rising from her chair.

That was the first time I had heard anyone refer to Otto by his first name. I wondered how Ada had come to know it.

"I hear the hay's in early this year," Otto called to her.

"I reckon it is," Ada said.

"Well then, if it's alright with you, I'd like to get in on it."

"I reckon you would," Ada laughed.

As Otto and the blonde walked into the farm stand, Wilson began rocking his hips.

"Ain't it a little early in the day for all that?" Otto Houser said to Wilson as he walked by the table, casting a stare over his shoulder at his son.

Wilson pumped his fist twice in the air.

"Sailor's salute," the blonde laughed, walking over to Wilson. The woman's jeans were short. As she crossed the parking lot, the fray exposed her behind. She smoothed a lock of Wilson's hair away from his eye and sat in his lap.

"Sailor's salute," Wilson said, as she settled into him.

"Afternoon, Callie," Ada said to the woman, pushing her chair out from under the table and spitting under her breath.

"Is it?" Callie said, leaning forward and pulling a pack of cigarettes out of the pocket of her shirt.

As Callie lit the cigarette, Wilson straightened up in his chair.

"Smokes," he said.

It was early in the day. Inside, the farm stand lacked its usual commotion. The hum of the freezer kicked in every now and again from the back. Cash had once tried his hand at the cattle business, turned loose a few meat cows on the muddy acres where the hay wouldn't grow. He'd marketed the choice cuts to a friend who distributed to the Steak House a few towns over. The leftovers he sold to the locals from the freezer out back of the farm stand. All that was left of the business was a yellowing sign, a hand-drawn image of a black and white cow with arrows pointing to the various cuts. The freezer now housed bars of ice cream and prepackaged cones, which Birdie and I bought with our quarters.

"Son," Otto Houser said, nodding at Fender while taking a sheet of paper from his billfold and laying it next to the register.

Fender stared down at the paper as though it were a speck of dust which he might as soon have blown off the checkout and swept under the counter.

"Seems Wilson's got a soft spot for that one," Ada said.

"Nah," Otto Houser smiled, nodding his head toward the patch of drive next to the bikes where Birdie was standing. "Wilson's taken a shine to the little miss."

"Poor thing," Ada said. "Can't help himself."

"Who can, Ada," Otto said.

A look passed between them. They both chuckled for a moment.

Outside, Birdie was eyeing Ada's empty seat at the table across from Wilson and Callie.

"Here, baby," Callie said laughing, holding up a checker, motioning Birdie over to the table.

"Well, what do you need then?" Ada said, turning back to Otto.

"My regular," Otto said picking up the list he'd taken from his billfold and handing it to Ada. "Seeing as the hay's early, I want to put an order in with Cash for a loft full of your finest."

"Well, there's nothin' that man can do that I can't handle," Ada said. "I'll put you down in the books for a truck load. Come on out back."

As Ada disappeared through the back door into the office, Fender plucked a honey stick out of the box next to the register and bit off the tip.

"I ain't your son," Fender said to Otto, spitting the tip in the dust and leaning back against the dusty pay phone behind the register.

Fender was the type of boy who grew up cat-spined and shady. Tall and fair and tow-headed, Fender could lean against almost anything and look like he was born to stand there, like he was made to do just that. I'd first seen him at school smoking cigarettes under the grove of birch trees that lined the fence. He wore a tight denim jacket and carried a brown paper satchel under his arm which I'd seen him pass around to the people he drifted with. Those days Fender came to school, he was suspended. At recess he was made to stand in the shade of the school building with his back against the brick. Watching him stand there, I remember thinking Fender could lean into the wind without falling over, propped up by reputation alone.

Lonesome for any visible parentage, it was well repeated that Fender was among the motherless, a legend which served to soften his fate. As the youngest Steelhead brother, Fender was viewed as the town's last opportunity to stamp out misfortune. When he lifted several volumes of encyclopedias from the local library, the librarians considered the books a donation. God willing, they said, Fender would read them. In the eyes of the town Fender was still open to redemption. Before the week was out, the library was missing the whole set.

Ada and Cash had run the farm stand out of their garage for as long as anyone could remember. When it came to troubled boys, they had seen the worst of them. Rumor had it, Cash felt guilty about calling the cops on Fender one night after he looted a patch of their tomatoes. To make it up to him, Cash had given Fender a few paid hours of work every week.

As I looked out at my bike parked in the drive, I wondered how Fender would answer the phone if it rang.

The list in my pocket was always the same with slight variation: an armload of zucchini, two peppers, an ear apiece of corn for us girls and two for Father. Though I knew it by heart, that afternoon as I retreated into the cool shade of the garage, I pulled Mother's list out of my pocket, walked over to the counter and placed it next to the register.

"Hey, Hotshot," I said.

I was wearing my swimsuit with allure.

"Well, what do they call you?" Fender said, deepening his lean and stuffing his hands into his pockets.

"Billie," I said. The name occurred to me on the spot. I'd recently taken to sifting through my parents' vinyls when Mother was out with the Separatists and Father was in the basement pining away over his college easel. Most of my parents' records were decrepit. They lacked the speed of the current moment. The one vinyl I listened to was the only one to which I could dance. It was electric and funky and sounded like it had come from some future generation. "Billie Jean" was the title track.

"Take one for the road, Billie," Fender said, pulling the honey stick from between his teeth and handing me the open end. I put my mouth over the stick and licked at the tip.

Otto looped his arm around my shoulder and brushed the front of my chest as though marking some kind of territory. "Get one of your own," he said to Fender before disappearing out back.

"Don't plan on it," Fender called after him.

5.

The hay wasn't the only thing growing early into the summer. That June, Father ordered a riding mower to keep up with the lawn. He'd been working overtime at Data General, the software engineering plant on Route 9. The riding mower came straight off the truck, factory direct. Being that we lived so far out of town, most items Father ordered had to be picked up at the Post. The rider was so large that UPS made a special delivery. The truck labored up the mountain. From a distance, I thought, it looked like one of the ready-made houses I'd seen tractor-trailers haul on the highway, the house expanding on the horizon the closer it came.

Father's rider came in a large cardboard box lined with a thin plywood plank. He kept the box in the garage until Mother threatened to return the mower along with it if Father didn't break down the packaging and take the refuse to the dump. The flower show was the following weekend, she said. The Separatists had ordered mums which they planned on storing in our garage.

The day after the flowers arrived, Mother went to church. The Separatists had organized a car wash after the service. The women, Father joked, planned on stashing the leftover cash for a trip to Palm Beach the local circular had been advertising.

The box was large enough that, side-by-side, Birdie and I could lie down in it. While Father was out mowing, Birdie and I snuck into the garage and made off with the box, carrying it on our shoulders along the riverbed to the far side of the marsh.

When we arrived, the green bottle was exactly as I had left it. Birdie and I dragged the box under the tree and cut a door out of the cardboard. I scored along three sides of the rectangular opening with Mother's gardening scissors and bent the box back so the crease served as a hinge. The rest of the afternoon Birdie and I gathered stones to mark off the perimeter. As we worked, the white branches of the birch crept into shadow. By the time we made our way up hill from the marsh, dusk was heavy along the horizon. Floodlights overlooked the back porch.

As we approached the Bottom Feeder, Father was playing the piano. In the background I could hear high-pitched laughter and the clinking of cans. I ditched the gardening scissors in the crawlspace beneath the garage and washed under the spigot, running my hands over Birdie's legs to scrub away the mud. Several welts were forming where the bugs had broken skin.

Together we stood on the back deck to survey our progress. If you leaned over the railing and trained your eyes along the riverbank, beyond the outer reaches of the floodlights, you could just make out the faint gleam of the rocks we had gathered, the white patches of mineral glinting in the dusk.

As we entered the kitchen, Callie was standing in the portico leaning over the piano. One hand on Father's shoulder. The other hovered over the songbook. Otto sat in the recliner in back of them. He kept time with his knuckles. A row of beer cans lined the cedar chest where Father kept his music. Father was singing a song about the things people needed.

"Join us, baby," Callie called to me in the doorway. "Your old man was just playing us some of his standards." Faded jeans rode halfway up her stomach. Her undershirt was pulled tight over her bra and tucked into the front of her pants.

"We've been out at the barn all day loading the loft," Otto said. "Your father invited us over to blow off some steam."

"Otto says he's heard you practice," Father said.

Otto smiled. "Play us something," he said.

I played the last piece in the book just as I'd heard it. Father stood behind me. Otto sat in the chair with Birdie in his lap. After the first several bars, Callie lost track and gave up on the pages. She sat next to me on the piano bench and hummed along. The piece didn't come with any words, just several repeating passages, which I played best I could remember.

"Wouldn't want anything to happen to an ear like that," Otto laughed when I finished.

6.

Otto called the next morning to say the Shetland was dead. Father set out across the road before sunup to help dispose of the body. Otto wanted to get the carcass in the ground before word made its way around the stable. "Found that pony lining its own stall when I opened the barn to put the feed out," he said. "Its nose still warm from breath."

When Father got home, Mother made him strip down and clean up outside under the spigot. They'd wrapped the Shetland's body in feedbags and buried it in Otto's south pasture, Father said. The old ceramic tub that had once served as a water trough marked the grave.

The image of the pony in the ground did not sit well with Mother. Lately, on nights when Father was sleepless and incapable of stepping away from the world, he slipped out the slider door onto the little deck that abutted their bedroom. Mother said she often awoke to Father's absence. In those moments, a strange stillness gripped her. The air was too light for her lungs. She could see the image of her husband's back on the porch in the blackness. Father took a pillow with him. The mornings after these nights, his voice was hoarse and scratchy.

"You sound faded," Mother said one morning at breakfast.

Screaming, Father said, released a chemical in his body that allowed his mind to find the emptiness in the world. Mother had mentioned Father's habit once, in passing, to Margaret and then regretted it.

"Dumping," Margaret said. "It's a psychological device like blowing up a bag and then popping it. The pressure deflates."

Mother wasn't sure what pressures existed in the country to be deflated.

"Don't look so alarmed, dear," Margaret promised. "To be natural is such a very difficult pose to keep up."

"Where's that from?" Mother had said.

"Wilde," Margaret said. "'*The Ideal Husband.*'"

"What else," Mother laughed.

As the summer wore on, animals of all kinds disappeared from the fields. Livestock were kept indoors to suffer the humidity away from the threat of airborne illness. During the daylight hours, the only forms dotting the landscape were the farmers in their flatbeds, the backs of their tires shooting up mud as they barreled around the fields to gather the bales of hay. The town grew quiet as people settled into an unspoken curfew. Even Ada took to wearing a straw hat over which she draped a piece of cheesecloth to protect her face from the bugs during those lulls in the game when she settled into sleep as Wilson fingered the checkers, mulling over his next move.

Callie was the only woman I saw disrobe that summer. Mornings Callie lay out on Otto's front lawn in her bikini before the day reached noon. The curve of her thighs and the flat of her stomach shone with oil. I passed the afternoons awaiting the sound of the occasional wood-paneled station wagon rumbling over the gravel, come to park at the base of the trail for a hike or a picnic over the butte. Even the milkman dropped our road from his circuit. If Mother wanted eggs, she had to send word via a form the postman delivered to the dairy. From a bird's-eye view, our town might've resembled Ada and Wilson's checkerboard; those people that moved did so with a worn-out deliberation.

Mother regarded the road with suspicion. She and Father sat in bed at night leafing through the local paper. To Mother, even the front page stories read like fiction. They reminded her, she said, of Birdie's first trip to the train station. We'd made the voyage to visit Granny Olga in the city. Mother had wanted to see her daughter baptized in the old church. In the elevator on the way to the platform, Birdie had pointed to a man standing next to her. "Mommy," she'd said. "Why is that man's skin brown?"

The elevator had been packed. There was no way the man had not overheard it. He shifted his weight, tugging on the edge of his suit jacket. "Country folk," I'd heard him say to his companion as they exited the elevator. "Haven't seen a shadow of the world bigger than their own two feet."

I spied on Mother in bed nights flipping to the last page of the paper to read the police blotter, looking for some texture of life that had survived the summer's suffocation. One evening she came across a headline about The Long Walker. She read the report aloud to Father: "Young 'ambassador cougar.' Seen by Nebraska Sowbelly. 23 Merriam Road. 6:30 pm. Attacked no humans or horses. Droppings consistent with Native Black Hills predator. Residents advised to keep pets indoors."

"The Long Walker," Mother said.

"What's that?" Father said, flicking the edge of his page so the paper collapsed in the middle, enough for him to see over it and into his wife's face.

"Nothing," Mother said. She paused for a moment looking at Father's eyes over the rims of his glasses.

"Have you heard of the Black Hills?" she said, tracing his beard with the back of her wrist as he nestled his hand between her thighs.

"Sure," Father said, "Some 2,000 miles west of here. Highest peaks east of the Rockies."

"That's quite a distance," Mother said.

"I'm more interested in these black hills," Father said, digging his hand deeper into Mother's lap.

The next day Mother drove Birdie and I out to the butte overlooking the highway while Father was at work. She parked on the edge of the cliff. Below the steep drop, cars sped by. The air had an industrial tinge to it, which Mother seemed to find comforting. She pushed the driver's seat into recline so that she could rest her feet out the open window and feel the breeze whenever a truck passed. As we listened to the sound of the trucks cresting the hill before the way station, Mother took out the old Atlas that she kept crammed in the glove compartment of the car for emergency. The Black Hills, she told Birdie and me while taking Birdie on her lap in the driver's seat, were an isolated mountain range that traversed from South Dakota to Wyoming. The trek east had taken the young ambassador nearly a year. As I looked out the window at the highway below, I pictured the body of the cougar as it emerged into the floodlights of Nebraska Sowbelly's chicken coop. Father often surrendered after work to nature documentaries on PBS. His favorites were about large birds of prey. Beyond the scenery, I wasn't much taken with these nostalgic glimpses of the hunt. What impressed me more were the strange feats of travel animals engaged in primarily for breeding. Birds flew south to the equator, migrating long distances called flyways, signaled by the length of the day. Salmon swum headlong upstream. Animals possessed honing devices that sounded at disparate intervals. This was something to which I sensed Mother could relate.

7.

Not long after the Long Walker was first sighted, Mother blew the house out. An awkward tri-level structure set at the bottom of a hill, the face of the house was blocked from view of the road by two trees of knowledge, trees which, by the time we purchased the property had abandoned their vertical thrust and grown into rooty, gnarled affairs—save for in spring when they vomited garlands of nauseating white blossoms.

The exterior of the house was made to resemble an English style country house, really a New Englander's version of an English style country house, a stately old salt box set amid sprawling beds of rugged wild flowers, thrifty crossbreeds that renewed themselves each year after the frost—both house and beds impermeable to any amount of cold or moist weather. Along with the apple trees, Mother called the house the Bottom Feeder.

"It opens up possibilities," Mother said of the blow-out plan, "In a glass home you are so much closer to the reality of the world." Modern living made life richer and deeper. She'd read it once in college in her roommate's copy of *Western Living* with its barefoot architects and 1970s California contemporaries.

Unlike the temples of glass and steel of which Mother dreamt, the Bottom Feeder had been built with the goal of providing maximum insulation and cover from direct light. The previous owners, the stencilers, had been elderly. On our first visit to the property, the man of the house sat in a rocker in the living room, smoking his pipe in front of the wood stove. The living room was lined on the inside with reams of cedar paneling. The heat of the fire and the humidity of the man's smoke fogged up the windows. For several months after we'd first moved in, the room smelled of wet wood and tobacco whenever it rained.

The exterior of the house was covered in a thick white stucco, a paint which, like the attitude of the house itself, retained a grainy, salt-and-pepper consistency. Occasionally, when you ran your hand over it, you discovered an unusually large blemish, a fly or two that had dried into the mix.

The blowing out of the house that summer was a family project. Mother hired a contractor to knock out the exterior wall of the house and install a band of modern floor-to-ceiling windows, large sheets of dual-paned glass, which she said would invite some of the outside world in. The contractor's team was comprised of several high school boys who stomped around the living room in tank tops and works boots, flexing and sweating to the radio. Occasionally, they went into the yard to smoke a cigarette with Mother. What the blowout plan lacked in insulation, it made up for in Mother's joy.

Once the windows were in, Birdie and I were given large soft-bristled brushes and sent to the sides of the house out of view of the road where the stucco finish had been abandoned in favor of wooden paneling, each panel thin enough that we could follow the grain and cover the entire width with a single stroke. When it came to painting, Father said the side of the house was all about getting on a good cover. Overlooking the marsh, appearance didn't much matter.

It was after a Separatist's meeting that the necessity of blowing out the house had come about. Birdie and I had spent a good part of the day at the Starlings', swimming in their pool. Ruth and Ray Starling were our closest neighbors and Mother's only friends on Fay Mountain, a fact established by proximity and common denominator; they were the only other couple under sixty living on our road.

Ruth and Ray had come into their marriage late in life. Ruth had lost her first husband early to heart failure. Ray's wife had left him when their children were grown. To their second marriage, both Starlings brought a horde of children and a fierce sense of autonomy. They smoked and drank and swore at each other. At the holidays, the whole brood shored up in one house and had it out over various cuts of venison that Ray had hunted.

Ruth and Ray were the only couple over fifty whom I knew to have a visible sex life. There was something of the tongue in the way they treated each other. Even when Ray was drinking and Ruth was yelling there was an intimacy between their bodies that felt comforting. Though age had left its indications—Ray had a case of beer tired around his middle, and Ruth blonded her hair—the pair were compact of body. After a day of mowing and tending the property, Ray would stumble, shirtless and sweaty, down to the pool where Ruth was watching us swim. The Starlings owned acreage. An outdoorsman and daytime drinker, one had the feeling Ray celebrated this fact to considerable advantage. At the end of the day, despite his sunburnt stupor, he retained a buzz and an eye for his wife's figure. This fact was known to anyone who visited them. Ruth often went about the house bare-chested, her low cut black one-piece barely pulled up over her nipples, the straps hanging loosely at her sides.

Those afternoons I spent with them, the two often retired around the pool in adjoining lawn chairs. After exchanging words, Ruth poured herself a drink from the bottle in the storage shed and returned to nuzzle her feet in Ray's lap.

Ruth was an RN at the local hospital. According to Mother, she assisted one of the young transplants living on the other side of the mountain fresh out of his residency in the city. Ruth was said to have delivered most people in the town and accompanied a good number of folks to the other side as well. A lapsed Catholic, she lent a practical eye toward good health and clean living. She dismissed the Separatists as new age voodoo practiced by thick-bodied women and closeted leftists. To Ruth, matters of the heart were an issue of protection. Ray himself said she'd married him on the off chance she ever found herself in a situation.

An ex-marine, Ray was scheming to avoid the order of the world. Bosses, like government, fit him like hand-me-downs. Most nights he worked late at his barbershop, a hole in the wall he'd set up on the corner of one of the little side roads in town where it emptied out into highway. He'd bought the place off the young couple living in the house next door when they were looking to finance their first baby. It had once been their garage.

Ray was a man who had lost his sport. What he had left of life was his gut, his gun, and the second woman he'd ever let into his home. With his first wife, he'd given birth to three incidental beauties. One in particular had that kind of drop-dead quality. At the holidays she was always bringing around men who seemed to slide off the couch and into her arms. Their suits had that cheap sheen. Bank managers. Owners of franchises. The last one I'd met sold pharmaceuticals and tended bar.

Ray claimed he bought his first Colt to protect himself those nights he closed up the barber shop. He never went far without it or his whiskey and kept a box of bullets under the sink in the kitchen. Father said Ray figured on protecting what beauty he'd brought into the world.

Unmoved by Margaret's invitations, that summer Ruth watched over Birdie and me more weekends than not.

There was something of the devil in Mother the night she ignited the blowout plan. It was dark by the time her Camry pulled up in the Starlings' drive. Mother beeped twice. This was outside the boundaries of her character. It was her habit to ring the bell or come in for a cup of tea or coffee. That night, she was in a hurry. Ruth shooed Birdie and I down the driveway toward the headlights. Mother hardly looked herself in the car. She had recently cut short her hair. Her long brown waves were now shorn in a modish bob that she blew straight and wore tucked behind one ear. Mother had the bone structure of an aristocrat and a tongue to match. Father said her nose alone could stop traffic. The recent cut seemed to take advantage of these assets. Under the porch light, she and the car acquired a certain celebrity. Together, they were waiting to shuttle us off to some greater fate.

The Bottom Feeder was dark as we pulled into the drive leading up to it. Mother had neglected to leave the porch lights on, her normal habit of protection. She said she liked to come home to a house that looked like it had people living in it. The three of us made our way down the gravel toward the house. The sound of the coyotes howling in the distance lending the air around us a vacuum-like quality. A knot grew in my stomach.

I clasped my hand around side of Mother and linked my thumb over top of her belt, fingering the pant loop. I felt the waifishness of her body, the hawk-like way her hipbones darted out from her skin as she walked. Despite all impediments to glamour, she wore belts that highlighted the trimness of her waist. That evening she was wearing the brown snakeskin with the brass buckle. She'd bought it with Granny Olga in the city.

The front door was unlocked. The bolt had caught on the frame, but hadn't yet slipped into the notch to secure the house. One push from Mother and the door swung wide. The foyer inside was dark. Mother's windows at the back of the house were open. A good breeze was coming in. Normally, the ventilation would have delighted her. That night Mother was quiet. I felt the side of her ribs expand as she drew in a breath.

"Get in the car," she said. "There's been a break-in."

The light from the Starlings' television lit up their kitchen. They kept a small portable on the counter so they could sit around the table and listen to the late night shows while they played cards. Mother was up the stairs before Birdie and I had time to catch her. "Get inside, girls," Ruth said, shuffling us into the house.

The floor around the table in the Starlings' kitchen was covered with newspapers. Bits of cut glass and foil. The air smelled of copper. Those nights Ray was too drunk for cards, Ruth had taken to craftwork. That summer, she was designing a line of lampshades.

"Sit down and make yourselves busy," Ruth said to Birdie and me. She removed several wire frames from the chairs and ran to the front of the house to call upstairs to Ray.

Mother was still on the phone when Ray was rummaging around under the sink in the kitchen. The back of his shirt glowed red in the thin light of the lamp over the table, one of Ruth's creations. He straightened up and slipped the revolver into the sheath which hung from his belt. The front of his undershirt was stained with a brownish liquid.

Mother came in from the living room. Her face was blotchy and bloated. She wrapped the phone cord around the palm of her hand.

"I'll just have a look around," Ray said.

Mother stared at his gun.

"I'm going with you," she said.

Birdie and I were asleep when Ruth drove us home. The house looked like a bomb had blown up inside it. There was a light on in every room. They'd turned the Bottom Feeder end over end looking for something criminal.

Father met us halfway down the drive. He and Ruth exchanged glances. He carried Birdie toward the house. I followed behind.

"I'll send her out now," he called over his shoulder.

Ray was in the living room with Mother. An ashtray half-full between them. Mother'd been crying. She looked at us as Father carried Birdie upstairs to bed.

In that moment, Mother appeared entirely outside of herself. The image of Father carrying Birdie up the stairs seemed at odds with her capacity. I often wondered if Mother would just as soon curl up in Father's arms than bear a daily maternal impulse. We were all fearful to admit this. On the outskirts of the town, Mother was removed from something vital.

"I felt some kind of disturbance," I heard her say to Ray.

The Amtrak station stood in back of the supermarket two towns over. It was the first of the rural stops on the northern route. The line originated in the city where Sterling had once taken up in the hotel. Ruth and I drove Mother. Nothing was said between us in the car. Ruth took a cigarette when Mother offered it. They smoked in silent communion. After that we listened to the static of the radio.

"It's just a little breather," Mother said to Ruth as she released the passenger side lock and stepped out into the parking lot at the station.

"Sure," Ruth said. Mother looked at me through the open window of the car. "There's a key under the deck in case anyone gets locked out," she said.

The tracks were dark. The train was not due into the station for an hour. Ruth pulled the car into the shadow of a dumpster to wait and watch. Mother stood in front of the board that hung in front of the station. She stared at the list of destinations, waiting for her number to come up. She was headed to the city under the guise of visiting Granny Olga. The flutter of the board seemed to help her locate some resilience. Here was evidence that the world was still churning. She'd just been outside the reach of its progress.

Mother had grabbed the old wicker traveler she'd brought to the hospital when she'd given birth to Birdie. She'd kept the suitcase packed so that she'd be *ready*, she'd told me, when the time came. Now she kept the case close to her body as she sat down on one of the benches facing the track. The station hovered, silent and anonymous. The yellow halogen of the Mobile sign next to the junkyard glared several streets over.

A pack of teenagers gathered on the bench next to Mother. For a moment I feared they would recognize her. Mother pulled her coat up around her face. I heard the crack of beer bottles where the teens hurtled them across the tracks. I was attracted to the violence of it. It reminded me of a gun going off. For months, Mother had kept the small television in the kitchen on the news. She was ready to be moved by a national story. I often wondered if she was searching the stations for her old flame.

When the teens had wasted all the bottles they started kicking around a hacky sack. I smelled smoke in the air and heard the familiar sound of a sack of beads where they lifted it from the ground. The bag landed not far from where Mother was standing. Mother shifted her weight. I remembered a story she had once told me about riding her bike to work one summer as a teenager when she worked the obit column for the Schenectady news. The city center was bustling and notoriously congested. She'd realized at once that her own survival depended on her ability to keep going. "It didn't help to stop amid traffic," she'd said.

A deafness gripped me as the train's engine halted. The conductor threw wide the steel door and descended the tracks. A scream erupted at the back of my head and flooded my eyes in one weightless, arid rush. I found myself opening my mouth and forming a hollow at the back of my throat as if I were about to release a long vowel sound the way Mother would when she reached for the high notes at church.

"All aboard, Ma'am," the conductor called into the darkness.

Mother clung to the railing as she mounted the stairs. It seemed as though her body hardly belonged to her.

8.

The morning after Mother's departure no one woke before noon. Father fumbled in the kitchen with bowls and boxes of cereal. Birdie and I poured glasses of juice. The three of us ate in the living room. Father put paper down on the carpet so Birdie and I could sit close to the television.

At that hour, the light coming through Mother's windows was strong. It cast a glare on the screen. Father papered over the window nearest the television with a few sheets of newsprint and some tape, shading the box so we could see.

It was break-back hour. By then we were Otto's boarders at the barn. Father'd bought that gelding that Otto had been telling him about. A flighty little Arabian. Not much more than fourteen hand. Green as hell. Still trying to throw the saddle. Otto called the horse The Sheik on account of his nervous side and his four white socks. "Reminds me of one of those Sultans over there in the Gulf. Nothing more than a bunch of snake tamers and criminals."

"Now that's the beginning of a good animal," he'd said of The Sheik the first time we saw him. "Headstrong. With a dose of healthy athleticism." It had been Sunday and raining. Father had driven the Bronco into the paddock where the trainer was lunging The Sheik on a long orange lead. In place of a vet, Otto had come with us to examine the animal and shake out any shadiness. The only thing that mattered, he'd said, was how a horse trotted out. The rest could be trained away or treated. "Horse people," he'd assured us in the car on our way to the stable. "Shy as hell the whole lot of them. Dog trainers. Now those bastards'll bury you in the quick."

After the trainer had trotted the horse several laps around the paddock, Otto got down on one knee and flexed the horse's front hoof in his hands, bending the joint back at the pastern.

The bottom of the horse's nail touched the tip of his leg where the hair shot out. He held the horse like this, putting some strain into the joint.

"Lame as a carriage horse," Otto had said to the trainer. "How much to take this dog food off your hands?"

As it turned out, The Sheik was a gravedigger. No space was large enough to appease him. At home in the pasture, he crawled the fences, circling the lot all day as if running the track. In the stall, he pawed furiously. We had to pad the clay floor with mats which stank each morning from the pools of urine. The only place where the shake settled from The Sheik's muscles was when you took him out on the trail. Confined by the brush and the branches, his body hurtled toward the opening in the trees as he steadied into a forward throttle.

The Sheik's was the only profile missing from the lineup the morning after he arrived at Otto's stable. When Father started into his stall for the bucket, The Sheik was hovering near the window, nosing at the rusty grate. His coat was matted and salted. The previous day's sweat had dried into peaks of crusted fur. The sill was thick with flaking paint and dried pigeon droppings. He licked the grate for salt.

"Knock on Otto's door," Father said. "Ask him for a carrot and a bottle of molasses. Anything sweet, if he has it."

Otto was a hobby man. What few interests he'd stumbled across in life, he wasn't apt to part with. Even the old junk he didn't quit easily. His porch was nearly full with broken machinery, stray chairs and random board games. An array of hulahoops and a pair of roller skates sat in the corner, amid the wicker porch furniture covered in a thin green mold.

A plastic hobbyhorse hung from the bike rack. Missing its spring, the horse pitched back and forth whenever you opened the screen door. "Callie" was spray-painted in silver script on its rump.

Wilson answered my knock.

"In here," he said in the odd hollow way his voice sounded once he got the words out.

I could smell His Helene from the doorway. Her stench had a full-bodied clinginess to it. The minute I entered the kitchen it invaded the inside of my nose and stuck to the fronts of my teeth so that when I ran my tongue along them, I tasted an acrid decay that I couldn't stop nursing on despite the impulse to retch. Even the kitchen itself smelled like an armpit after a night of anxiety and sleeplessness, a mixture of sweet onion and old wound.

His Helene had her tail up. The house was in heat. Everyone in it was facing death ass-first to the wind. The haze of morning hadn't yet lifted. The curtains were drawn and the windows were open. What little light there was in the room existed only when the wind blew open the drapes creating nervous patches of light on the wallpaper. If it weren't for the glow of the switch on the coffee pot, I would've thought I'd woken someone.

"Bath time," Wilson said.

His Helene emerged from the bathroom. She appeared no thicker than one of the strips of light on the wall. There was so little left of her to hold on to that Otto seemed to carry her without notice, her arm draped over his shoulder as her feet dragged beside him on the carpet. Her frame could've easily been mistaken for a trick of the eye created by some movement of the curtain. Her gown hung open exposing several growths on her back which reminded me of the way roots stretch when the earth starts to erode: shallow, spread thin for air.

"What you lookin' for, Petunia?" Otto called over his shoulder to me as he steered His Helene toward the bed that opened out from the couch.

"Sweet stuff," I said. "The Sheik's off his food."

"In a minute," Otto said. "Give me a hand."

His Helene never said, "Hi love." Or, "Come join us baby." What she said was, "So, you think you can play. Otto says you think you can play me a sonatina."

"You've got your rot on, Helene," I said. Her bed overlooked the south pasture where Father helped Otto bury the old Shetland. The south pasture got the afternoon light. "Wake me up when I'm bronzed," she said.

"My Helene," I said. "You're crispier than burnt bacon." Really, it was the jaundice. She was nearly glowing with it. "A slow leak," Otto Houser explained it. "Hole in her stomach."

"Red hots," I said as I removed the bedpan and wiped her down, looking for signs of sores or sudden bouts of perspiration.

"Kidneys," she called them.

"That's my girl," Otto Houser said as he spread her legs and arranged her body.

The salve he used was thick and oily. He showed me how to thin it with the friction of his palms.

"Easy does it," Otto said when the grease was the right consistency. He lifted His Helen's legs exposing her bottom. I spread a layer of ointment over the patches of red.

When I had a good coat on her, Otto handed me a small white pellet.

"Let me show you," he said taking my hand in his and gliding the pellet up into his wife's crack.

As he withdrew my hand from the warmth of her body, he ran the length of his finger under his nose.

"Smell her," he said.

9.

Mother wasn't the only one holding her tail high that summer. What I noted most about her absence was the pheasant farm. The doctor had erected a coop on the corner of his property where it met ours. His birds strut around the fields in back of our house, noiseless, stubborn, brimming with pride. I watched them out the windows Mother had installed which looked out over the deck. Nightwalkers. Daywalkers. His birds were both. They had no respect for the hour of the day or the confines of their dwellings. There was an arrogance to their beauty that I found both attractive and abstinent. The way they hefted their legs and cocked their bright heads towards the sky, they were always stepping over something as though the very ground beneath them were rotten.

We bordered the doctor's run on the north east corner of a thickly wooded pine forest. Our scrub and shade was stopped short by a stone wall and a tangle of barbwire. On the other side of the wall lay the doctor's plot, acres of pristinely plowed land on which he housed fields of corn or wheat or alfalfa depending on the season. How these fields were kept up or by whom, no one could fathom. The doctor remained more myth than reality. Every now and again word went around that he'd taken a new vehicle, a signal of distant prosperity. People would've blamed such a man if it weren't for his offspring. His wife housed pregnancies like ritual. No one could turn their nose up at a man with such seed.

The doctor's fields provided a straightaway where Father galloped headlong into an empty expanse of green and wind. In Mother's place, Father purchased a seventeen hand Morgan named Rebel who used to pull carriage and wasn't yet used to the weight of a man. In the barn, Rebel was all pussy, nosing your crotch for scent or your pockets for grain. As long as you were under foot, he let you blow your scent in his nose. Under the saddle, Rebel was all riot. He'd try to throw it the minute you tightened the girth. The way he hung his head reminded me of those big broad shouldered men who'd never harnessed their athleticism and rather stooped around always looking for a woman's back to glide up on and adhere to.

The Sheik and I were often at Father's heels as he spurred Rebel across the doctor's acres, squaring off with what pieces of the world he had left behind. Father rode in an old red and white bicycle helmet. The thin red chinstrap flapped wildly around his face in the breeze.

Evenings after Mother left, Father turned to his creative habits. For Father there was nothing alluring in the newness of progress. An engineer, he felt betrayed by the achievements of his profession. Data General may have been the wave of the future, but for Father, computers merely allowed one to operate in a language outside the banalities of human circumstance.

"I've still got my girls," Father often said to Birdie and me after dinner, pushing aside the furniture in the living room where the three of us could lounge. Our nightly games were played this way, soldiers in the field.

The bald spot on the back of Father's head glowed in the track lighting as he bent over the piles of Pick Up Stix, contemplating his next move. Father believed that when it came to strategy, one could win if you just understood the physics.

Birdie often grew bored of waiting for Father to take his turn.

"Try that one," she'd say into his ear, climbing on his back and pointing over his shoulder at the stick buried deepest in the pile.

"Just a minute, kiddo," Father would say. "We've got to consider this problem from all angles."

Afterward I retired to the Atari while Birdie ran jumping courses over stacks of pillows she'd piled in the doorways of the Bottom Feeder. Birdie'd adopted an old hobbyhorse as her mount that summer, thrusting the wooden handle between her legs and galloping off into the foyer while peering ahead at the jump in earnest. Whenever she knocked a pillow down, a look of discernment came over her face; she'd slap her thighs and cluck her teeth to egg the horse onward.

Father surrendered to his sketchbook or an episode of *The Joy of Painting*. When forced, he would catch up on work in front of the cathode ray monitor on the desk in the corner of the living room. The monitor weighed a ton, and could only display sixteen colors. The next year, with the birth of the World Wide Web, Internet access would be as slow as boiling water. The modem would beep and hiss until it made a connection. For now, the three of us lost ourselves in a session of King's Quest unawares of the greater world around us. You were constantly having to save the game, as it often forgot your progress. Even the most useless items encountered on the quest—a dead fish, a rotten tomato, or an old board—could have an unexpected and creative purpose in the right situation. "When a situation looks completely impassable," Father said. "A good idea is to leave it and come back later."

Above the computer hung a painting of Father's. A modernist construction. Four multicolored sticks set on a deep blue background. The canvas itself was long and vertical—taller than Birdie or I—and it took up most of the backdrop to the computer. The four rectangles overlapped one another at various heights, as though magnetically attracted. I often stared at the rectangles wondering which I would remove first.

"What do you make of it, kiddo?" Father would say to me, wrapping his arm around my shoulder in front of his masterwork.

"It's got symmetry, Pop."

Before bed we snacked on Cheese Nips and Slice 'n' Bake. Birdie ate the cookie dough straight out of the wrapper. Those nights we ordered Chinese food, Father made us virgin Scorpion Bowls out of Kool-Aid and cans of fruit salad.

Dr. Who was the only program on which we could agree. We enjoyed the blue police box which became his space ship and tumbled into the galaxy. There was something about this arrangement that seemed plausible that summer. We watched the show in solidarity.

Father, Birdie, and I sat cross-legged with our backs against the couch, which Birdie had stripped of its cushions. "What's your name?" Dr. Who says to the girl as they run to evacuate ship. "Cas," she says. "You're young to be crewing a gunship, Cas," Dr. Who says. "I wanted to see the universe. Is it always like this?" she says. The two stand on either side of the door and yell passionately at each other as they part. "I'm not leaving this ship without you," Dr. Who calls out to her. "Get out of here," Cas says. "While some of the universe is still standing."

10.

During the day while Father worked, we were watched by a train of women.

Our first girl was a bleeder. The daughter of a psychologist and one of the women who worked line at the cafeteria. She lived in a small Cape close to the center of town. Those mornings I'd seen her standing at the foot of her drive as the bus rounded the corner, she looked like the sort of star who'd wasted the fetch of her youth trying to settle down with some country boy who'd loved her and left her. In his wake, she'd taken to hitching her way across America to understand just what it was the rest of us were doing. I expected her to stick out her thumb when she saw the bus round the corner.

Our bleeder was not a regular. The driver kept a look out for her. Those mornings she was running late, just exiting the small door of the house as our chariot pulled into view, the girl moved down the drive at a slither, her leather clad arms full of bags and bangles, not a book or proper paper weighing her down. Once aboard, she disappeared down the aisle of the bus. We left the last seat empty for her next to the Emergency Exit. We figured her for someone who bet on solitude to make her happy until she found her way out of this place and into the big thing for which she was meant.

Her name I never was clear on. Everyone called her something different. It was one of those headliners which had a purr to it—Katerina, Katya, or Katelyn—the derivative of some family name which must've belonged to a distant grandmother. Luckily, she was the type of girl who lent herself to nicknames and variations—Katie, Kathy, Kat. I just called her K, as in the letter, because it was easy to remember and it allowed her to be whomever I wanted her to be on that particular day or hour.

The first night K arrived I understood that Father was meeting Mother. I could tell by the closeness of his shave, the way he tucked and bothered. K had driven over, a move Father usually would've declined as he always drove our girls. This evening when K arrived, he'd barely looked at her, his usual attempt at conversation replaced with a nervous fidgeting around in the kitchen for his wallet and his keys. "These them?" K said, pulling out the clunky iron ring from under a stack of newspapers on the counter.

She held the ring out in front of her. When it came to keys, Father wasn't frugal. He had an eye for lock boxes and bike chains, anything that could be secured and then unsecured through a series of numbers that tested logic. Father never threw out an old key because he could never remember what it belonged to. There was probably a key on that chain that unlocked his dorm room in college. I figured it for the small, three-toothed brass.

Once he was gone, K and I were left standing in the kitchen. She eyed herself in Mother's windows as she crossed into the living room. Though she wasn't overly thin, she moved with a balletic confidence.

"Do these things open?" she said, nodding at the window. She stood on the back of the couch, undoing the upper lock.

"We usually keep them closed," I said.

"You get that one," she said.

Once the windows were cranked, she smoked a cigarette overlooking the deck.

"Some fall," she said, leaning out for a moment.

The fact that it was her duty to entertain us, seemed to eclipse her. I was taken aback by her pause.

"I've tried them," I eventually said.

"Really," she said. She exhaled and let the smoke linger. "I never figured you for a smoker."

"I've watched Mother," I said. That was true. There was something about this statement that seemed to soften K.

"Well," she said. "It's never too late to quit."

She finished the remains of her drag, pinching and flicking the stink out the window. The rest of the butt she carried through the kitchen and flushed.

I retired to my bedroom to scheme. Eventually I came down to check on her under the guise of getting a glass of water from the kitchen. She was sitting in the dark watching television eating slices of ready-made dough. The way the contours of her face lit up in the flicker of the screen, her beauty struck me not only as a presence but a talent.

I lay in bed waiting for Father's return in a strange incapacitation. I watched the various levels of darkness come into the room, training my eyes to detect the slightest change in gradient, which signaled the approach of a car. When Father pulled into the drive, the pattern of the headlights on the ceiling seemed comic-like in their amplitude. The dim beam of K's own headlights followed as she backed into the road and pulled away.

I waited for the sound of any movement on the stairs, the slow, deliberate shuffle of Father's feet signaling that he was once again retiring alone. In the silence, I half anticipated Mother's bound. Mother functioned in only two speeds. Her body shifted imperceptibly between the loll-and-graze and the dart-and-skid. I'd watched her lithe frame passing Father on the stairs one evening before she'd left. She'd angled herself between his hip and the railing so as not to interrupt his march. Instinctively he'd reached out to trap her, circling one arm around her waist. He'd held her there, taking the back of his free hand and spanking her. She'd struggled in his arms. They'd shared a long kiss at the top of the stairs.

"I'm wiped," I had heard Mother say in Father's ear.

"Not yet, you're not," Father had said.

That night Mother had on a short nightgown when she came to tuck me in. I'd seen her wear the nightgown when applying her makeup on those rare nights she and Father were going out. I'd admired the neckline and the thinness of the straps on her shoulders in the bathroom mirror from where I sat on the counter the way women admire each other when they're alone. In the thin light of the hall that evening, as Mother had bent over to kiss me goodnight, I could see the curves of her thighs where they separated between her legs and the patch of hair between them.

That was the first night I'd heard my parents engage in their respective yearnings. Just as I was about to find sleep, I'd heard the clang of the headboard, which I recognized from those mornings Birdie and I jumped on their bed. I would have thought little of the noise had it not been for the rhythm. Its persistence would die out for a moment only to return with a louder, faster gait.

After a time, the rhythm was punctuated by a loud calling out. Mother's voice erupted into the darkness. Its pitch reminded me of the high notes I'd heard her reach for in church. There was something sad about this noise. I used to imitate it on the walks I took to the marsh after she left. In the woods, it sounded lonely, the sort of call a bird would make to her young to signal her return to the nest with her kill.

The morning after I'd first heard their love making, Father had soft-boiled eggs, which he'd crushed in the bowl and ladled with butter and salt. Mother'd fried slabs of toast, which she'd soaked in milk. The bacon was thick with fat and grease. I'd lined the plate with paper towels to catch the run off. What I remembered most about that meal was the laughter and the sound of the music on the stereo. The low notes were muffled as the speakers were small and old and failed to capture much range producing a tinny carnivalesque sound from what other-wise would've been the smooth depths of Southern jazz. A box of Domino sugar had been left open on the table. By the end of the meal, it was nearly empty and we were all giddy with food and high on one another.

That morning, under the cover of my parents' enthusiasm, Birdie had escaped the task of clearing. As I'd headed from the kitchen to join her, I'd seen Mother glide into Father's arms, pressing him up against the counter near the sink. She was carrying the sugar bowl and wearing a thin pair of white shorts and a tank top through which I could see the outline of her nipples. As she'd moved into him, he'd parted his legs slightly so as to accompany the wale of her. Before I'd turned the corner, I saw his hands trailing the shape of her body until they reached the curve of her breasts.

"Your mother is a beautiful woman," he'd said as I'd passed them.

The night Father returned after the first of K's watch, the only sound trailing him was the whine of the refrigerator and the click of the light in the front hall as he turned down the switch. I awoke in the night to footsteps pacing the hallway and the rattle of ice in a glass.

As I descended the staircase the next morning, Father was sitting in the old club chair in the living room. The chair had been positioned so as to face the television. From Father's stillness, I thought he'd drifted off while watching the late nights, until I realized the screen was blank.

"It's just me, Pop," I said, not wanting to surprise him.

The way his eyes looked in my direction and then drifted, he seemed hardly to recognize me, any sign of acknowledgment in his face or his posture replaced by slack jaw and glaze. His cheeks and the broad expanse of his forehead had lost their hue. Even his features looked shrunken.

I stood in front of him for several moments hoping he'd adjust to the presence of life in the room.

The light that day was excruciating. The sun blasted through Mother's windows with the kind of brilliance that bleeds landscapes of their color. The rug lost its grain. The room felt empty and cube-like. Everything in it appeared balded and gray.

Looking at Father with his back to the row of windows, when I shifted my head various parts of his body disappeared in the glare as though through them I could see out the window and beyond. Beyond him I imagined the image of Mother beneath the apple trees in the yard sowing the bed of begonias which lined the stone wall where our property met the road. Her skin was tan and leathery. Her breasts bounced as she bent over where she was not entirely buttoned up. She worked from the waist, pulling up small patches of green where they had raised their heads above ground. An ant climbed the inside of her leg. "Look at all these cues," she said, straightening up for a moment, surveying the rows of wild flowers that shifted in the breeze. Inside her, I saw the reflection of the window at Father's back. If I looked into it I saw into her stomach, the small pit where she kept all her food. I could taste the bits of roughage—dried apricots and bites of asparagus—mixed in with acid that had made its way down into her stomach from the hollow of her cleft. When I looked through it and beyond, I saw the old ceramic tub across the street where the Shetland was buried in Otto's field. When I stood in that spot, a good clean breeze ruffled the back of my hair.

"It's not as bad as it looks," Father said from his chair.

11.

When it came to private property, the Steelhead brothers taught me everything I know. They lived alone in a big brown house on the top of the mountain. According to local legend, they were fatherless. What they saw of their mother was what time she had between men. It was said they killed dogs in their basement. Rumor had it, they even tried killing a pony once. Tethered it to a stake in back of their house and watched as the pony walked itself in circles until it dug a track so deep it walked into the ground.

What I knew of the Steelheads' story I'd gleaned from hearsay and what I'd observed from our front door. Each Sunday, I'd seen Mrs. Steelhead's Impala clamor its way over the gravel and up the drive. Her hair she kept wrapped in a towel piled on the crown of her head. She came with some regularity and always at this hour, the hour of morning when the night was just burning off and the sun was rising over the road. Her Impala moved at such a clip that, if I nodded off, I feared I might miss the site of her gunning it up the hill.

One morning before Mother left us while waiting for Mrs. Steelhead, I had nodded off in my sleeping bag in the front hall. Mother had stumbled upon me on her way downstairs for breakfast.

"Who you waitin' on, Jean?" she'd said, taking my feet off the tile and rubbing them between the palms of her hands.

"Mrs. Steelhead," I'd said.

"Mother of three boys and the woman rolls home Sundays at six in the morning," Mother'd said. "I bet that hussy's still wet."

I remembered this now, as I made my way toward their house.

The Steelheads' dwelling sat in a small clearing in a densely wooded knoll at the top of the mountain. More pothole and frost heave than surface, the road took a good bit of leg just to manage the weave. Macadam flew up under my bike wheels, nicking the backs of my legs. I avoided the big ruts for fear of getting a flat.

The house itself wasn't the ramshackle structure I'd imagined. It looked like the first in a long series of houses that populated the new breed of pre-suburban developments: the fantasy of an old turn of the century carriage house standing on the foundation of its character and convictions, but recreated with a skeleton of new plywood and plaster. In premise, the layout embraced something of the great wide open. There was air in the rooms. Even a good deal of light. Somebody'd had money once. Somebody'd once proposed trying her hand at familial structure. Someone'd once wanted to care for these brothers.

They had a Lazy Boy, an old braided rug of the sort I'd seen in Grandmother's house where the dog laid in the kitchen, and a big screen TV. Beyond that, the house lacked furniture and decoration. The front rooms were empty save for a few cardboard boxes and a large inflatable palm. The tree functioned as a punching bag. Here was WWF, monster trucks, and a sanatorium of white walls. Someone had punched a hole in the bathroom door.

The elder Steelhead boys had nothing of Fender's wit or charm. Tall and dark-haired, there was a shiftiness to them I distrusted, a raw meanness that comes from experiencing some rupture in human dignity. History was afoot in that house. That stale acrid thing which eats children from the inside leaving the outside to blow around without consequence or intention like a dried out husk. Some days the brothers were harmless, their menace reduced to ghostly indifference. Others, they were entirely flammable. To add insult to injury, Fender's looks eclipsed theirs. This made them a shade meaner.

Fender was the first person to call me on the phone. K was watching us that day. It wasn't her habit to answer the phone when it rang. I kept a list of calls on the sticky notes. When it rang, I had to run for it.

"It's me," Fender said as I was about to hang up.

We met at his house. I told K I was going to the farm stand for dinner. I arrived at the Steelheads' looking for evidence. Dogs in cages. A pile of horseshoes. The remains of the pony on the chain who'd walked himself into the ground. What I saw were the relics of an old blue and white motorboat decomposing in the glen to the side of the drive. The only evidence that lived up to legend was what looked like an animal run, a small stake in the ground with a metal chain. As I walked toward the porch, an old collie nosed at my leg.

Fender met me at the door. "Do you want a soda or something?"

"Sure," I said.

The kitchen was the gut of their loneliness. Half-eaten bags of Utz chips and beef jerky occupied the majority of counter space. Boxes of Muscle Milk and packages of Creatine were stacked in the corner. Near the basement door there was a large black garbage bag. Several flies buzzed around its mouth. The refrigerator was empty except the bottom two rungs, which were lined with cans of generic soda. I went for the cream. When I opened it, the cap popped, unleashing a current of fizz. Instinctively I put my mouth over it and guzzled. The eldest boy, Liden, was yelling at the wrestling match on the television. He barely blinked as Fender and I crossed the room toward the stairs.

Fender's room housed two single beds fashioned from cheaply varnished pine. The beds were shorter than they should have been for a boy his age. We sat at the base of the one in which he slept while Fender showed me his collection of cards. Father never had much interest in scores or teams. I wasn't sure how to react to such men's things. As Fender listed off names of the players, all I could think about was the thickness of his sheets.

Here was the boy who smoked cigarettes on the playground still sleeping between spaceships and stars.

"They're a bitch to crack," Fender was saying when I regained focus. He was talking about his collection of geodes. "You never know what's inside until it's broken."

"I've never tried," I said.

"Limestone," he said. "The best spot to go looking is the stone wall. There's so much you trip over it." Fender got up from his bed and walked toward the window, pointing toward the stretch of wall that lined Otto's pasture.

"Let's go," I said.

As we turned to leave, Liden stood in the doorway.

"Quit it, man," Fender said.

"No worries," Liden said. "I can see you've got company."

"Leave her alone," Fender said.

Liden eyed me for a moment then laughed.

"How about that new video game?" he said.

"Maybe later," Fender said.

"Just one game and I'll let you go," Liden said.

The hallway to the attic was dark and stuffy, padded with tufts of insulation. As we made our way up the stairs, Liden trailed behind us. I imagined him grabbing me the way I'd seen Father grab Mother on the stairs. There was something thick and oniony on Liden's breath.

"You were right," he said to Fender in the darkness. "She's nothing but a baby."

The attic was lit by a single exposed bulb that hung from the ceiling. In one corner there was a small television. On the floor beside it was a mattress. Piles of videos and magazines were strewn about.

"Have a seat," Liden said.

We took our seats on the mattress and flicked the television on.

The thing about porn is that it's nothing without the windup. Without the story or the stripping, it's all just a mess of appendages. I'd seen horses rear up on each other similarly in the paddock. Two geldings sparring over a mare. Though I understood the violence of it, the sexuality for me was missing.

"Let's see you two go at it," Liden said. He gripped my knee on the mattress from where I sat between them. With his other hand he tugged on the fray of my cut-offs. "I'll watch. You don't look like you're built for two at once."

Fender leapt over my body and pinned Liden on the mattress with his elbow, crushing his nose with one of the controllers. Liden rolled away from me in pain.

"Go fast," Fender said, grabbing my arm.

"You get home safe now," Liden yelled down the stairs after us.

Outside, Fender and I sprinted through the woods in back of the house. Fender picked his way through the underbrush. By the time we reached the stone wall we were walking. He'd mined this spot before. A small wooden shelf built of two-by-fours was nailed into a tree. It held a flashlight and a toolbox. A red crow bar and a thick handled ax leaned against the trunk. In the space next to the wall there was a patch of earth devoid of grass. This was his splitting spot.

Our first day was a gutting. It took Fender nearly an hour to split anything off. We were hoping for a clean break down the middle. By the time darkness set in, the wheelbarrow was lined with small boulders.

"Get in," Fender said. I sat perched on our pile as he pushed.

We made our way down the long drive that led to the Bottom Feeder. A breeze rushed over the flat parts of my face. Every now and again Fender let the slope of the hill take the wheelbarrow and I felt as though we were gliding. He chose the grassy part of the hill next to the drive where the ground was soft and even. The sky had on the kind of hue that precedes certain sunsets in the heat of summer when even the air is tired, all shade having burnt off by the end of the day, revealing streamers of violet and blood orange.

We unloaded the rocks onto the gravel under the spigot in front of the house. K's car was parked in the drive. In the thin light it looked like a tin matchbook car which I might press with my thumb and roll down the hill into the marsh. As Fender dropped the last stone in the pile, K appeared on the front porch. She peered down at us.

"Where did you two get lost?" she said.

Fender looked up at her under the floodlight. His undershirt clung to his chest. Though he was significantly younger than K, you wouldn't have known it to watch him.

"She was with me," he said.

"Ain't that the truth," K said, pulling the edges of her sweatshirt over her chest.

We saw two beams of headlights on the horizon.

"You better be getting on home," K said, nodding at Fender.

"Take mine," I said, nodding at my bike where it was laying in the drive.

Together K and I stood on the porch and watched Fender disappear up the trailhead. Under the stoop of his stature, the frame of the bike looked dwarfed and circus like. He had to lean over the handlebars and stand on the pedals to steer. The white of his T-shirt and the rim of the bike's fender glinted in those places they caught the light. I followed them until they disappeared in the wood over the top of the mountain.

12.

The next day Father went fishing with Ray. That morning the house sprinted into the world. I woke to the sound of Father crashing about the crawlspace in the basement looking for his pole and box of tackle. Night was still in the air and with it that impermanent glimpse of other seasons with their welcome respite from the sun and the heat. Father had put a pot of coffee on in the kitchen. The dim yellow light shone over the stove when I came in.

"Who knew a man like that had ever seen the right side of six a.m.," Father said as Ray powered down the engine of his truck in our driveway, relaxing in the cab for a moment to smoke the last of his cigarette. Birdie and I carried bags of ice onto the lawn. Ray tore open the bags with the back of his switchblade. He unloaded several six packs into the row of coolers closest to the tailgate, stirring the ice around with the back of his hand, burying the bottles under the frost.

"When those brews are gone, Rick, what do you say we fill those coolers with bass?" Ray said.

"I'd say you've outdone yourself, Ray," Father said. "I like a man who outdoes himself. I'll be back with the cold cuts and bread. We might have a hankering for something hearty out there."

As the two men made eye contact, Father chuckled, running his hand under the visor on his temples. Father was a man who spent most of his life trying to cultivate a ready laugh. Though he was built like a workhouse, when it came to conversations, he had more of a dancer than a boxer in him. "Back in a minute," Father said, jogging up the walk to the house.

"Good man," Ray said, with that sportiness that came from years of playing football and working in the army. In his eyes, no man who knew the burden of having a wife and kids was outside the purview of an honest day's fish.

That day, I was to spend the morning with Margaret. Birdie would stay at home with K. Mother had made arrangements from the city, Father said. Ray was tight lipped on the matter. The bed of the truck loaded, he slammed the tailgate shut and I jumped into the cab.

"You sure you don't want to come with us, lady?" Ray said, as he hoisted himself into the driver seat, shutting the door and turning the key to the ignition. "We've always got room in the dinghy for a deckhand." "Mother arranged for me to spend the day with Margaret," I said.

"So I hear," Ray laughed. "Do me a favor. Tell her your old man and I went fishing without a license. That should give her something to rail on for a while."

I looked at him for a moment. For a barber, he had a rough face. His stubble was gray and patchy. There was a thin grease in his hair, which appeared rumpled from the last place he'd run his hands through it. Despite the hour, his eyes were alive and fresh. I could tell there was nothing malicious in his jest. He was a man who woke on the right side of circumstance and liked to lend some of his humor to the day when he could.

"Scout's honor," I said.

Father emerged from the house. He fumbled with his keys in the lock before hustling down the walk toward the truck. He'd slung the old army backpack that he and Sterling used to take hiking over his shoulder. Father was always naming off the mountains they had peaked together. "As boys," he'd say.

"Jeanie," Ray said chuckling. "Be a lady and jump into the back to make room for your old man."

I moved down the bench toward the center of the cab in order to swing my body over the rise of the seat, upsetting a loose stack of newspapers next to Ray.

"What are you hiding under there?" I said, brushing aside the papers. Ray's Colt sat on top of a cheap low-gloss circular advertising the week's specials. Home goods and electronics.

"You never know when you'll find a sand shark trailing you in the water," Ray said, taking the gun and focusing it through the windowsill in front of him. "Don't want any predators sneaking up on our big game." He narrowed one eye as though picking off a fish as it leapt from the water.

I looked through the windshield in front of us. Father started to run toward the truck.

"Jesus, Ray," Father yelled through the window. "Put your gun away. That's my kid you've got in here." Father's voice was making that jagged pant it did after he'd galloped Rebel.

"No harm done," Ray said. He opened the door to the glove compartment and tucked the Colt under a pile of napkins. "I wouldn't be caught dead on the open water without some form of protection." Father slid into the cab.

"She'll be safe in there," Ray laughed slapping Father's thigh before starting the engine.

The back of the cab was narrow and dirty. The floor was littered with work shirts, random utility tools, and empty cassette cases. I sat on a pile of newspapers stacked behind Father. The seats in back were short and squat. They flipped down from the walls. The rocks and dust kicked up around us as Ray sped off. The road had that type of lonely exhilaration.

As we passed the Starlings' home, there was a light on in the kitchen. A creature of habit, Ruth kept her husband's hours. She'd gotten up to put a pot of coffee on before Ray'd left for the fish. I imagined her sitting around their kitchen table in a thin pink bathrobe fingering a pile of cards, savoring one of the lone Parliaments she kept in the back of the junk drawer behind her make-up and the piles of bills.

The road followed the curve of a short steep hill. At the bottom sat the Young residence. Ginny was a nurse in the children's ward at the local hospital. Dan kept house, an arrangement which was widely suspected but rarely spoken of. The renegade son of the local construction company, Dan had abandoned his share of the business. He'd thrown off his Father's shadow in favor of Vietnam. He'd returned from the war with a back injury that kept him from steady work. Dan kept a motorcycle and a small fishing boat, which he financed by working odd hours at the auto body. Occasionally you'd see him working in the driveway, fixing somebody's carburetor.

Something in this arrangement would've irked people had it not been for Dan's service and the beauty of his wife. Petite and naturally trim with a perky bosom that she showed off while gardening in her two-piece, Ginny had a doll like quality which made men like Father clam up when they spoke to her. People respected Dan for having the courage to keep her around. Such a task required that a man of his means be around on the constant. Dan and Ginny had produced two children. Lissie, Danny Jr. and I rode the bus. The town was not required to fetch us. We offspring of an unpaved road which dead-ended at the town's border walked each morning to the little bridge near the farm stand where the dirt met the pavement. We waited for the bus on the stump next to the stop sign at the corner. If we were early, we raced sticks under the bridge, a habit Mother had warned me against as the bridge was preceded by a blind turn around which the occasional car came speeding.

My experience of the Young's house was based on a single exposure. I'd been invited to dinner once when Mother had class at the feed store and Father was working late. Lissie had prepared a casserole while her father slept on the couch in front of the game. Danny struggled with a load of colors in the basement. A chart of chores on the refrigerator was evidence of their father's regiment. Despite the abundance of foil stars, bright red and blue assigned to Lissie and Danny respectively, the refrigerator gave the kitchen the effect of Christmas in the barracks of an underground war unit, the iridescent stickers glinting in the light of the overhead halogens every time anyone opened the door. When Ginny returned home from work, her lips were still glossy. Her eyes were the only thing that betrayed her. The brilliant blue replaced by tired blinders of gray.

At the table, Dan Sr. had said grace. It seemed we'd barely stopped eating when the children were up clearing and scraping. A bungalow built in the style of the frontier with a large triangular atrium and a sleep loft that overlooked the kitchen and living area, the house itself boasted the slick and sleaze of a seventies ski cabin where people from the city went to drink bourbon and turn down the sheets on one another's' wives for a weekend before stumbling back into their Rolls, the fridge still stocked with dark winter brews and the carcasses of half eaten chickens. Here were the glass windows Mother dreamed of. I imagined Ginny luxuriating in front of them each evening after a long day of making the rounds, slowly undressing herself in front of the wall of glass that looked out onto the street while Dan watched from the couch, her thin chemise slipping down around her ankles to reveal her gentle curvature, which she pressed to the window, bending over so that through the part of her legs Dan could watch for the flash of headlights as they came up the street as Ginny made love to whomever might come to pass.

Meanwhile, the kids were tucked into their dormers at the rear of the house at an early hour. Lissie laid on her back and breathed heavily through her nose. Danny engrossed in a monster truck magazine illuminated by the small screw-top flashlight he kept under his sheets where he would eventually keep a switchblade and later his first gun.

The bungalow's distinguishing feature was the flag Dan Sr. had erected on a tall metal pole on the front lawn. The girth of the pole intimated the seriousness with which Dan took this project. Erected in a small round bed of concrete around which the grass was mown, the flagpole was treated with the reverence of a monument. Each morning Dan walked out onto the lawn, barefoot and winded, with his eyes lifted toward the sky. Not a man to be rushed, he fixed any fold or snag in the flag's fabric before raising the stripes to their full altitude where they billowed for the road to revere.

That morning, we'd caught Dan securing the line when we drove by. Recognizing Ray's truck as it lumbered down the hill, Dan waved, eyeing the hitch and the boat in back with envy. "Good man," Ray said as we barreled by, saluting the flag through the window. A fellow man of the uniform, Dan came to attention. Ray chuckled. "Crazy bugger," he said under his breath. "Now there's a man who knows how to keep his luck around."

Beyond the Young's house, down the road a stretch, was the stop sign where Lissie, Danny Jr. and I waited mornings, the little bridge in all its earnestness, and then the beginnings of Ada and Cash's fields, their gray shingled house, and beside it the farm stand.

The streets skirting the radius of town were decorated by the types of homes with driveways that ran in a horseshoe and were lined in a reception of old town cars. Pillared porches and tall white fences enclosed trellises of wild roses and pots of imported tomatoes. Here decadence shifted in perennial storm. In winter, when the flowers and the tomatoes were under snow, images of horses in gingham blankets speckled the landscape. The lawns of these homes were turned into pastures where horses were kept close to the houses. Occasionally, the animals would run to the front of the yards and cast their necks over the fences, whinnying at the cars as they passed.

In the center of the town was a green with a gazebo where people were married. Around it, pillars of New England gathered in silent communion. The library with its green clock face. The Inn that housed the old tavern. Steeples and bell towers of every denomination. Next to the Congregational church sat a legal office, a tearoom, and a country store. Occasionally, Birdie and I rode our bikes to the store and bought Pop Rocks and Candy Cigarettes with change we collected from the tin under the kitchen phone.

Margaret was sitting house for the young, recently widowed lawyer whose office was in the center of town. Margaret said our lawyer was suffering what every man faces after the death of his wife: the prospect of many sleepless nights bookended by two days of solitude. Weekends, for him, were marked by the occasional meal at the pub and the sound of the dog's footsteps crossing the wooden floor of the kitchen in the morning before begging at the door to be taken out. The lawyer still kept up with his parents whom he often visited. Margaret, his neighbor and sister in solitude, watched his house. Despite the depth of its character, her own studio lacked the yawn and stretch of a true home in which the soul could forget itself between doorways.

As Ray pulled into the drive, Margaret was outside watering the begonias. She'd tied a white scarf around her straw hat to keep it steady as she worked. The brim shielded her face. When she moved her head the shadow muted the sharp cleft of her nose and the harshness of her cheekbones. In one hand she was slung an old watering can. In the other, a metal trowel, which she waved at me as I walked up the drive.

"Have her home by six, Margie," Ray yelled out the window as he backed into the road.

"Always a doll, Ray," Margaret boomed back at him. "Save me that bass this time, if you catch one."

As Ray's truck disappeared down the road, Margaret turned and started up the walk.

"Let's put lunch in the fridge and have a swim," she said. "I like to get all my work out of the way in the mornings when I'm still good for it."

The kitchen was open and light. The sun streamed in over the large cast iron sink illuminating an island of wood over which hung a collection of cookware.

"I'll chop," she said. "You give these a wash."

The salad was a cobbled together affair. Lettuce chopped into thick wedges, strips of bacon left from breakfast, and a handful of strong smelling cheese. Margaret smoked as she worked, resting her cleaver on the edge of the cutting board every now and again for a drag on her cigarette.

There was a distance to her silence that I appreciated. After the vegetables were chopped, we went for a swim.

The pool was long and in-ground. Strings of buoys were set up in lanes. Margaret removed her hat and her sarong, draping them over the fence post before heading to the deep end where she dipped her toes and then dove. I watched her swim several lengths. The oval of her back moved down the pool at a steady clip. When she reached the end, she curled into a ball and flipped under water. The backs of her heels were the only parts of her which displayed any evidence of exertion. They blushed a slight red as she pushed off the wall.

I put my arms over my head and dove in to the lane next to her. I paddled in a rough breast stroke, an awkward choppy necking which involved a few strong pulls punctuated by the occasional scissor of the legs. I could never stave off the feeling of drowning.

Afterward, we sat in the lawn chairs and dried off. There was a slight breeze. It dried the hairs around my temples. When I ran my fingers through them, I felt a tug where the roots pulled on the skin. Margaret tied her hair back with one of the thick rubber bands from the post office. She kept a stack of these around her wrist.

"Well then," she said. "Let's have a nap to revive ourselves before lunch."

She put her hat over her face as she slept. Every now and again when she let out a low breath, I glimpsed at the chair where she was reclined. Margaret's body was a solid raft which didn't slumber out around her. Her breasts were modest. Small canonical hills that rode close to her body. Nothing about her outsized humble geometry.

I grew tired and lay back in my chaise. When the sun hit, my body warmed at even integers. After a while the insides of my lids were lit a bright yellow, which burned when I stared up into them.

I woke to Margaret tapping me on the shoulder.

"I must've drifted off," I said.

"Are you getting enough sleep nights?" she said.

"I've never been good at it," I said.

We lunched on the veranda next to the pool. The meal was punctuated by the occasional passing of the water or the chirp of a chickadee in the distance. Margaret kept a small white mug in her hand on which from time to time she tapped her ring. It was filled with a dark liquid I figured for coffee. She sipped it as we ate.

Afterward we retired to the darkroom, a makeshift studio in the bathroom of the hallway off the mudroom. For Margaret there was nothing secretive in the way images revealed themselves. The beauty of developing lay in the science of the chemicals and the way a body moved in a dark space. I sat on the back of the toilet and manned the wash. "Not such a bad day for an old lady," Margaret said, holding up a large black and white image of the young lawyer diving into the pool. "What do you think of this one?"

In that moment, I realized Mother had passed countless hours in this space. Here her presence was felt even in absence. It surprised me that Margaret had not mentioned her. A painful awareness was let back into the room. Mother would've known just what to say about anything. Here I was holding my tongue.

"I've never been much good at diving," I eventually said.

That night Margaret drove me to the Starlings'. She took the back roads. Her old white Volvo, with its wooden stripe and bullish head, flew down the hill out of town. She drove in the center of the road with no regard for sides or lanes. With the wheel she took a light touch, switching hands often to tap her cigarette. I put my arm out the window when we took the curves.

Ray's pickup was parked in the drive when we arrived. The two men were on the back porch.

"You're forgetting something," Margaret said as I opened the door of the car. She reached into the backseat and handed me the dusty black body of the old point and shoot we'd practiced with that afternoon.

"Here," she said. "Next time, we'll develop some of yours."

There was something definite about the weight of the machine in my hands. I slipped the camera strap over my head, righting its body on my chest.

"Sure," I said.

Father and Ray were on the deck as I came up the stairs. Their backs to me, the two men stood side by side looking out over the yard. Ray was teaching Father how to shoot. "Loosen your grip and let your wrist do the work," Ray said.

I paused as Father released a round over the pool and into the clearing. A metallic smell hung in the air. Ruth emerged from the kitchen with a tray of rock glasses and a bottle of Scotch. Father and Ray startled at the sound of the screen behind her.

"Where's all your fish?" I said.

Father turned to look at me. I glimpsed a light in his eyes, a reflection perhaps from Ruth's lampshade in the window. As he bent down, it flickered and went out. I reached up to him. He picked me up in his arms and pulled me to his chest.

"Let's get you home," he said. "I bet that sister of yours is knee-deep in trouble."

My legs knocked against the Starlings' railing as Father carried me down the stairs to the truck. I was too big already for carrying.

The sun set over the hill as Ray drove Father and I home. The bed of the truck behind us smelled of sweat and fish. The stink came in through the windows.

"Wreaks to high heaven," Father said.

"Keeps the coyotes away," Ray joked. "They've been kicking up a storm. Woke me from the dead last night. I went out on to the porch and heard this yelping. It sounded like it was coming from over your direction. By the time I got my gun, whatever it was had wandered off."

"Poor sucker," Father said.

"Next time," Ray said. "He'll get what's coming to him."

13.

Fender turned me into the kind of girl who was always tearing the clothes off her body at the first sign of running water. "Hold up, little bug," Father'd say those nights I came home from the clearing. "Stop all your buzzing. You'll confuse the flies."

The day after Father's big fish, I was waiting for Fender at the start of the drive. The smell of bass in the morning is enough to make anyone go running into the world. Father was sleeping. I scribbled a note for him on a napkin and left it in the kitchen under the glass duck where Mother'd once stashed notes to Father those nights she was going to be late at a Separatist meeting.

"You're early," Fender said when he arrived.

"Stunk out," I said.

"Well," Fender said. "If your funk gets too thick down there in the clearing, you might have to go bathe it off in the stream."

The previous week we'd flung ourselves headlong into a stealing pact, pilfering Liden's collection of dirty magazines. Fender'd come down one morning with a bruiser. Liden had gone on a hitting streak. K and I iced Fender's eye with bags of frozen peas. We made him promise he'd sleep it off in the basement.

Fender and I were going to paper the box by the marsh with cut outs from Liden's magazines. Fender'd been slipping them out of the attic one by one since the bruiser. Each morning he brought me a few glossies: monster trucks, and *Sports Illustrated*, and some of the harder core stuff, which he kept at the bottom of the pile and told me not to be alarmed about. "That's not for papering," he said. "One night we'll build a bonfire and blaze this smut."

"Sure," I said. Smut sounded like it would burn.

Fender was leaning hard on something. "Dad's home," he said. "First time since last time."

"When was last time?" I said.

"Oh," he said. "When Mom went on a cruise with her pharmacist. Said he came around to watch over us while she was out fucking. Admitted to liking us a little bit even."

"You're a likable lot," I said. "Minus your brothers."

"Mostly," he said, "I think he came back to clean out his things when she was out of his hair. Now he's on us about the house."

"Is it his?" I said.

"I don't know," he said. "He left it to her when he split. Payoff for his mistress until he found out she had her own on the side. Now he lords it over her whenever he's short on money."

"Maybe they're fighting over custody," I said.

"Nah," he said. "At this point we probably belong to the state."

"Refugees of California," I laughed pointing at an ad for surfboards on our box.

"Right," he said. "At least it's better than Michigan. Michigan never had any thing other than a lake."

"Well," I said, "At least you could row out into it if you needed to make a break for a while."

We abandoned the bikes in the sand next to the mailbox and packed into the marsh on foot. Every now and again Fender gunned me with one of his half-smiles. When the wind picked up, I thought I smelled a trace of cologne he'd lifted from his father.

At the bridge, he smoked a few cigarettes while I rummaged around under the trees picking my sprinters, short narrow twigs with enough heft to get picked up by the current but without the girth to create friction with the undertow. I won twice of my own merit.

Fender lifted a small golden bottle out of the pocket of his bomber, which he said he wore to protect his arms from the brush, but really I knew he was keeping his bruises hidden.

"What's with that?" I said.

"Nothing," he said.

He took a few swigs, more nosegay than fire. It made me sad, this kind of trying.

"You don't need any," he said, when I reached for it.

"How do you know what I need?" I said.

It didn't take long before the box from the rider was gleaming. Elmer's glue, monster trucks, beaches with girls with all their womanhood in the chest. According to the front door, Winchesters were on special. We clipped the ad for surfboards that boasted the slogan California Dreamin', and posted it on the rear wall above the little window I'd slit.

The box was big enough that we could lay side by side on our backs with our legs stretched. Fender had stripped down to his shorts. He bathed his T-shirt every now and again in the stream and tied it around his neck.

"Take that thing off," I said. "Before you flood the place."

"Just you make me," he said.

I straddled his middle with the thick part of my thighs while batting around at his head trying to undo the place where his T-shirt was knotted. The move was a holdover from childhood games of wrestling with Father. Father had said he didn't want me to turn soft like him.

Fender was swift but I had the advantage of his sleepiness from the liquor. I had him by the wrists. We paused like this for a minute, his arms out in front of me, raised up above his head. His chest heaved. I looked him in the face.

"Not bad for a light weight," he said.

We struggled, my forehead cupped in the palm of his hand, the weight of my body blazing down into him, until a head rush set in.

"Uncle," I said, and he released me.

I crawled off Fender's body and lay on my back beside him. I pulled the front of my T-shirt out of my cut-offs and wiped the sweat from my eyes.

"You're taking up all the air," Fender said quietly.

The hair under his armpit brushed my neck as he slipped his arm under my head.

I slid my hand down the front of my jeans, pausing to be sure he was watching. As I stared up at the sky, I made small circular movements with my hand. The birds chirped and Fender was silent as he watched. I thought of the young girl in the barn, the day she had showed me. She'd laid down in the hay stall one afternoon and spread her legs. She was wearing a pair of thick white tights with one of those circular crotches. Her hand moved around inside it.

Afterward, I went over to the tree where I'd hidden the rucksack. As I bent over to readjust my hair, I felt a sting on the back of my legs where Fender flicked me with the wet part of his T-shirt.

"Got yah," he said, sprinting past me up the trail out of the marsh.

When we emerged onto the road Otto was having it out with The Sheik in front of the barn. The Sheik had witnessed a great fright in his youth. The sound of water in a gutter ten feet off made him stop short. Otto was trying to train the nervousness out of him. There was a thick sheen to The Sheik's coat. His legs frothed under his tail. Otto spurred him forward, trying to get the horse to stand with his hooves on the grate in front of the barn where the runoff from the mountain emptied out into the sewer.

I admired Otto for the way he rode with his hair gleaming. Helmets, he said, were for novices and women. I'd heard him tell Father that saddling a horse was like taking out the mother of your children. You combed your hair and dressed for the occasion. Rumor had it, Otto'd trained horses for the Kennedys once.

The Sheik stared unflinchingly at the sewage grate across the road as we approached. His front legs were squared. Otto let him have it on the head with the blunt end of the whip.

"Flighty devil," Otto said, stroking The Sheik on the withers once the horse was straddling the grate. A thin sweat had broken out on Otto's brow. He dabbed at the moisture with his hankie.

As Otto dismounted, Callie made her way down the drive.

"Jesus, Houser," Callie called. "You break my balls just watching."

"Why don't you take this flighty little Arab out jumping while he's good and greased," Otto called to her. "He'd fly over a barrel of burning petrol if you asked him."

"He's more of a lady's ride anyway," Father said.

"The old show boat," Otto said. "Sides of iron. Soft as hell in the mouth. Doesn't like other men hanging on his beauty."

"You know what they say, baby," Callie said, gutting the foam from the corners of the horse's mouth where it had gathered around the bit. "A feather in the saddle is a bird in the hand." She smiled at Father.

"I'll give you a leg up," he offered.

I remember the rise and fall of Callie's bottom as she trotted off down the road toward the far pasture where Otto had set the jumps. It was that time of the day where the shadows grew long and dusky. What was left of the sun existed somewhere between the curve of Callie's behind and the saddle. We all stood there admiring it for a moment.

"Haven't known a horse that hasn't taken to her," Otto said.

As we turned the bend toward the paddock, Birdie came up the road. She carried a small metal tray lined with Dixie cups. Watching her approach in the setting darkness, it seemed the world would swallow her whole. She'd spent the day at the Starlings' under the care of their eldest daughter who was trying to convince her suit, the one in pharmaceuticals, to give her a baby. In the meantime, she was borrowing other people's children to show off her skills.

"What have we got here?" Otto said, kneeling down to examine Birdie's tray.

"Mouthwash," Birdie said. "Two for a dollar."

"Well now," he said.

Birdie put the tray down in the road and reached into her pocket. She produced a wad of bills.

"Where did you get those?" Father said.

"Ray's daughter sent me out with them," she said. "She said I could keep a dollar for every ten."

We stood there staring at the wad of green in Birdie's fist wondering if Ray's daughter was back on coke and needed money.

I looked down at the rows of Dixies. The mouthwash had saturated a few. A thick blue liquid seeped onto the tray.

"Well I'm no stranger," Otto said, reaching into his billfold and handing Birdie a ten dollar bill. "I'll buy you out. You didn't do anything wrong."

Otto took a cup from the tray and shot the liquid into his mouth, swishing for a minute before spitting into the grass.

"Not bad," he said to Father. "Toothpaste and club soda."

Callie was making the rounds by the time we reached the gate.

"Jumped three foot fences since the first time I threw her in the saddle," Otto said watching. "I've never seen a woman more alive with her feet off the ground."

"Some people just aren't made for walking," Father said.

"Never was. Never will be," Otto said. "Problem is, she doesn't have an eye for a husband that can hold her anywhere but half way down his nose."

"Well," Father said. He looked at me for a moment before pulling me to his side. "You know better than all that," he said. "Tell me you know better than all that." Father's eyes were glassy. He was talking about the Dixies and the coke and he was talking too about the light under Callie's rear and how much he both feared and admired it.

We stood watching Callie jump until there was enough dusk in the air that the oxers had lost their color.

14.

After all the light had faded, Fender and I bore our hides. The phone rang as I was clearing the dishes.

"It's hot up here," Fender said.

We met at the Starlings' pool.

I raced him there panting and gleaming. I'd given myself a good scrub in the shower, looking for some ugliness to shed. What I found was a mound of flesh at the top of my thighs and Mother's plastic razor rusting in the corner of the stall.

It took me a while to figure out which way to go with the hair, to shave against the grain.

Fender hurdled the fence. I climbed the chain-link hand over foot. Once, I thought I saw a light go on in the Starlings' kitchen when I rattled the links.

"Stick close to the shadows," Fender said. "And don't let your mind get the better of you."

"OK, Senator," I said. "Don't get ahead of yourself."

Our stripping off was a hurried embarrassment. There wasn't much glamour in us. Mostly that part of him just looked like something best left under his trunks. His shoulders were everything. Broad and smooth and tapered, they anchored an acreage of muscle which moved easily under his flesh.

Once we were in there wasn't much to do but move around. The water was cool. The willow which overlooked the fence cast a shadow on the surface. We kept what parts of ourselves we could submerged to avoid drawing attention should anyone come to a window. Every now and again I felt the pull of Fender's body as he swam by. There was something confident in his small undulations.

"I wish we could go sliding," he said, looking up at the big blue plastic shoot next to the pool.

Eventually I got out to shake off. There was nothing to do but drip. I stood there with my arms out. The night was warmer than the water. I leaned over and wrung out my hair. A puddle formed around me on the concrete. Fender paused under the willow.

"Quit staring," I said looking for the whites of his teeth, wondering if there was a smile for me beneath all that.

As I bent down for my clothes, Fender hoisted himself out of the far end. There was something shy in the way he approached me. He girdled himself up in the middle and shielded himself with his hand. I'm not sure if it was his age or the tendency of a man to hold himself close in the cold, but there didn't seem much to cover.

When Fender was dressed we sat in the chaises. The crickets were out. Fender looked restless. Our big baring had let him down.

"Well, at least we got to swim," he said.

I wanted to keep him out longer by the pool.

"I know where Ray keeps his bottle," I said.

We jimmied the lock to the tool shed where the Starlings kept their floats. Fender dropped his jackknife. It made a dull thud on the concrete.

"Keep a look out," Fender said.

After that we were in.

The whiskey was under the oilcloth Ray kept over the generator. I reached for the highball glasses off the shelf next to the goggles and dusty mouth tubes.

We filled the glasses half way. Fender was planning on stealing the bottle. He fiddled with the inside of his jacket like he wanted to put something heavy against his lungs.

"Nah," he said after turning the whiskey around in his hand for a minute. "It wouldn't be fun that way."

The first sips burned. A flame leaked down the back of my throat. After a while I started to taste caramel. Maybe it was the color. I opened my lips and tossed back my head.

When our glasses were empty we sat there staring. Fender's eyes dropped down his cheeks when I looked at them too long. My head felt heavy for my neck.

"Put it between your knees," Fender said. He brushed my hair out of my face. I kicked over my glass. It shattered on the concrete. The lights flicked on in the Starlings' hall. We had the time it would take Ray to bend down under the sink in his stupor to retrieve his Colt.

The first shot went off as we hit the bushes. Ray was aimed high to scare off the coyotes. It was too dark to kill anything from such a distance. Even still, you never knew where he'd point his piece.

"Fuck," Fender said. "The cops will be all over my place."

"Ray's a drunk," I said. "They'll probably just think he did it himself. If not, Ruth will blame him."

"Why would a man steal his own liquor?" Fender said.

"Maybe he forgot where he'd hidden it," I said.

When we emerged from the woods, we sat on the old boulder that lined the road in front of the drive to the Starlings' house. The old blind guy in the golf hat lived there with his fat wife. Sweet people too. No one ever heard much of them. The man drove an old yellow Volvo. Occasionally he took it out when his wife wasn't home. I'd seen him rushing headlong down the wrong side of the road. He had that old people way of taking life on the offensive. People said he kept the boulder at the end of his drive so he'd know when to turn. Father'd gone over once in a storm. The snow had been so high that it took out the electricity for several days. The fifth day, Father got to worrying. If the old couple perished, he'd feel responsible. Mid-day he put on his tall rubber boots. Mother gave him cans of baked beans and creamed corn. When Father returned home he said the couple had been living on Spam and soda crackers. The old fatty had tried heating soup over a candle.

"You think they're alive in there?" Fender said looking back at the house. The lights were off. Given the hour that didn't mean anything.

"I don't know," I said. "Just be careful not to trip the flood. Father says they've got a light system on that house to scare a criminal. The old guy waits until the cat trips the alarm to get up to piss at night."

In the distance we heard a group of people coming down the road. Father was among them. I recognized the way he lumbered. When he walked he kicked up half of the dirt in front of him. This is what they mean by kin. You see yourself most clearly in them when they're just a speck on the horizon.

Otto was with them too.

It was odd to see people out at that hour. Summer had a way of dragging part of the day into the evening. There was so much heat to be had.

Fender and I hid behind the boulder until they passed.

"I'd pick them off if I could," Fender said, lining his arm on top of the rock and cocking his finger.

"That's my old man," I said.

"Your old man keeps some company," he said.

Wilson was holding up the back of the line next to Callie, the heels of his trousers dragging in the dust. Cash had brought along a few of the farm hands, migrants workers whom he kept on through the picking season. Father and Otto were the first to pass. They dragged an old horse blanket full of brushes and equipment. I recognized it from the print. It belonged to the Shetland that had died. With his free hand Father was smoking a cigar.

"I'll pack it in when we hit the brush," he said. He nodded up the road where it dead-ended into the trail that cut into the forest and let out onto the butte overlooking the highway.

"I knew there was a reason I spent so much time hanging around a young man," Otto said. "Almost makes up for you stealing all my women."

"I haven't stolen anything yet," Father said.

"A woman can only put out her signals so many times before she gets tired of waving her flag around," Otto said.

"It's a losing man's battle," Father said.

"The problem with men your age," Otto said. "You've got your eyes trained too far ahead. You get so caught up in all this dying you've got left to do, you forget to get up every day and shave your damn beard."

"I like my beard just fine," Father said.

Otto clicked on his radio, an old transistor that he used to listen to the ballgames. "I hope the rain holds off till we get a good burn going," he said.

Fender and I started to trail them as soon as the men were out of earshot.

They settled in the clearing overlooking the highway where Mother, Birdie, and I had sat while observing the Atlas. The sound of passing cars at that hour was nothing but the occasional screech of tires. There was a traffic light a half-mile off in the distance where the highway met the interstate. Next to the on-ramp was a weigh station for the truck drivers and the drunks.

Fender and I crouched in the bushes. The men built a fire in the sandpit. Fender said his brothers and bunch of the high school kids went there to make out on the weekends. They'd built the pit to roast hot dogs. Someone had constructed a grill out of an old bike tire to toast the buns.

Father tossed the tire to the side while Cash cleared out the pit with a rusty rake. One of the kids who frequented the spot must've brought the rake out there to tame the fire at the end of the night after everyone'd gotten sick of getting off.

Once the pit was good and level Father and Otto doused the Shetland's blanket with kerosene. Ray tossed the match. The men's faces lit up as they stood watching the flash.

"Stand back," Otto said as Wilson started toward the flames. "There's enough sickness burning in there. I've seen enough death this summer."

Otto set the old transistor on the end of the picnic table closest to the pit. He kept Callie's shadow in the corner of his eye. The legend was Callie'd come to him as a child. Otto'd started her in the stable as a favor. His Helene had insisted Callie live in the RV with Wilson. By the time Callie was legal, she'd shown the best horses in the county. Along the way she'd found herself a husband. It was unclear now where she slept nights. She'd turn up for days and then disappear for a stint.

That night Callie belonged to Father's loneliness though he didn't know it. Once the fire was burning, Otto turned up the music and got everyone on their feet. Even Father danced. Callie moved into his arms. Father stared at her and tried to pattern his body after hers. The farmhands retired into a huddle around the fire with a pack of Coors. Someone produced a bag of peanuts. Occasionally you heard the crackle of a shell exploding as they tossed it into the flames.

The remains of the Shetland's gear burned into the evening. Though the body was cold in the ground, Otto figured there might be some disease still lurking in the earthly possessions to which the horse once belonged. Disease crept up out of the earth that summer. No one wanted to see any more of it. Especially Otto.

Just when talk had stagnated Ray emerged from the brush. He fired a round into the air on the other side of the clearing. "Pellets you animals," he cried when the men started hollering at him. "Just thought I'd bring a little noise to scare off the coyotes."

Ray was drunk. Otto and Father each took him by an arm.

"Dumb fuck," Fender kept saying. "I should have stolen his bottle just to spare his wife half her hassle when he gets home." It was cold in the bushes. Our feet were damp. The liquor had dried out the inside of my head.

Fender shivered in his shirtsleeves until I put his arms around me under his jacket.

"There," I said.

"So this is what old people do to get off?" Fender said, pulling me closer. "Light fires far enough from their homes that they don't burn their wives down?"

I drifted off to the vision of a carnival. I was riding the old white hobby horse hanging on Otto's porch. The music from the merry-go-round was loud and the smell of popcorn hung in the distance. Each time the ride made a turn my little white horse lurched forward. From the way it sounded when I tapped my fingers on the body, I could tell it was hollow, nothing but empty fiberglass. Just as the ride let out it started to burn.

I woke in the night to the sound of two men urinating in the bushes.

"I never meant to want much from her," I heard one of them say. It sounded like Father. I wondered if he was talking about Callie. I wondered how far he'd fallen for her. I wondered if he'd pulled her into him as he'd done that morning with Mother in the kitchen.

The next morning we woke to the sun in our eyes. There was dew on our faces. Everything around us was wet. Fender was on his feet with a cigarette. I wiped the dirt from the backs of my thighs. "I'll get you home," he said. "Before they come looking."

I walked over to the pit where the ashes were smoldering and extinguished the embers with my foot. The whole place smelled like whoring. It was the horsehair or the kerosene. I tapped the corner of the Shetland's blanket with the corner of my toe to stir up the last of the coals.

At the bottom of the pile there was a small metal bit. "Dead weight," Otto had described the old snaffle to me once. "Barely pulls any at the corners. Every now and again you massage his tongue with it to remind him to turn. When an animal takes to gumming the metal, he's already broken. Best thing to do is turn him out to pasture and let him cut his teeth on the brush."

He was an old pony that Shetland. I remembered how easy he'd taken it in the mouth.

"It's too much," I said to Fender as he came up behind me.

"What is?" he said.

I looked at the ashes still lighting up off one another in the fire pit and thought of the remains of the old Shetland decomposing in the pasture. And of the bodies coming home from the Gulf whose names were announced on the news. And of the eerie quiet of the Bottom Feeder in Mother's absence. The games of Pick Up Stix with Father on the carpet. The empty couches surrounding us stripped of pillows so Birdie could build her jumps like trenches in the doorways. The house itself looked like something had exploded from within.

"All this warring," I said.

15.

Callie kept a frozen chicken in the cupboard over the sink. The flesh was stacked on the pile of china next to the whiskey and the boxes of bullion. She kept a Styrofoam tray wedged between the plate and the bird to catch the runoff from the thaw. It took a day for a bird like that to shed all its ice.

The evening after the bonfire at the butte, Callie'd invited us to a meal. Birdie and me and Father along with Callie's husband, The Little Wrestler, and their three young brutes. It was late in the afternoon by the time we arrived. The previous night was still heavy on us. I could tell Father felt it too. "You look tired, Jeanie," he said as we got out of the car. "Why do you look so tired?"

We gathered around the table in Callie's kitchen and watched her prepare the meat. Never has a woman performed such surgery. She massaged that carcass like she was trying to resuscitate some old heart. After each cut was slick with dressing she floured both sides with cornmeal.

"Test the fryer for me, baby," Callie said to me, motioning toward the pan. "Toss a little water in with your fingers and see if it sizzles."

We were there under the auspice that Father knew something about pipes. There was a clog in her disposal. Callie said one of her boys had stuck an action figure in it again. "They're trying to replicate war," she'd said, motioning toward the battlefield enacted by the G.I. Joes in the living room when we'd come in. The disposal had produced a realistic mangling to the leg.

"What do you make of my handiwork?" Callie's husband said to Father as he entered the kitchen. "I was just under there a few days ago."

"A fine job," Father said from where he lay on his back with his head under Callie's sink. "I've never been much good with my hands. Just thought I'd lend an eye to it while you were out."

"Don't they teach you professor types which way to turn a screw in law school?" the husband said.

"Rick's an engineer, Rod," Callie said looking down at Father as he pulled himself out from the cabinet.

"That explains why he's fixing my drain pipe," the husband said.

He laughed then. "Next time she'll bring a damn preacher to teach our sons to shoot hoops. If you need me I'll be out in the yard with the animals."

Rod let the screen door go behind him as he made his way into the yard. It slammed a little on its hinges. The spring was still tight.

"Why don't you put all that away, Rick," Callie said gently. "I'll get you a clean towel."

"I suppose it would be good to freshen up," Father said, brushing his hands against his knees as he righted himself in the tight space of her kitchen, ducking so as to avoid the low-hanging lamp.

Callie handed me a plastic spatula and motioned toward the chicken where it fizzled in the pan. "Let them golden," she said. Father followed her down the hall toward the bathroom.

I watched Rod through the window over the sink as he made his way into the yard. There wasn't much anger in him. He had a flatfooted way of walking which betrayed his low center of gravity. According to Otto, Rod had been a wrestler. Callie had met him while he was out on the circuit. "Back then she would follow anything around with a Harley and a helmet," Otto had said. "First it was the rock bands, then the bikers. Eventually she landed with a crew of wrestlers who frequented the bar where she worked. Rod was short. It was all she could do to show herself off to him."

The way Rod shot hoops now with his sons you could tell Callie had taken the lay out of him. He had that short guy's way of aiming high so the ball bounced off the backboard and rebounded on the front rim before meeting the hoop. He tossed one after another like this. I'd seen carpenters nail a board with more energy.

Their house was a one-story ranch. It sat back from the road on a plot of land next to the commuter highway. An old swing-set floundered in the front yard. One of the swings was broken. They'd strung it up with the chain. In back there was a tool shed that Rod had turned into a barn where he kept a few chickens and a small brown cow. In front of the barn he'd poured a square of blacktop at the end of which stood an old basketball hoop. Several dirt bikes were parked in the knoll under a tree.

Birdie was outside on the blacktop with Rod and his sons.

"You get too close to the thing," Rod yelled as the largest of the boys landed under the hoop, bending backward and hurling the ball over his shoulder with a clumsy underhand. While the boys shot around, Rod took Birdie up on his shoulders. Every third throw he'd walk her over to the hoop and let her shoot. She reached for the rim like she wanted to hang for a minute. One of the older boys came over and lifted Birdie up under the arms until she was standing on his shoulders. He stood under the hoop while she lunged. She made the catch and hung like that for several seconds, pumping her legs.

Down the hall Father ran the water in the bathroom. As the faucet clicked off, Callie called out to him. "I'm in here if you need a towel." Father followed her voice. I could hear him lumber into the hallway and down the hall a few strides. He paused and then turned. I waited for a few minutes, listening to the chicken fry. The flesh was still pink in the middle, not yet cooked through. I put the lid on and slipped down the hall after Father.

Father had left the door to the bathroom ajar. The window above the toilet was shaded by a curtain covered in a layer of dust. The bathroom itself was from another era. Thick yellow tiles lined the backsplash. The linoleum around the sink was worn and brown in patches. A canister of room spray glowed a sea-sick green where it was plugged into the wall. The muted blue acrylic of the shower stall—clearly a recent addition—shone in contrast to the faded seventies veneer. Around the mouth of the tub was an assortment of plastic action figures. A single naked Barbie hung upside down from a string around the spigot. I wondered which of Callie's young brutes played with the doll in his bath.

I flattened myself against the wall and peeked around the corner. Beyond the doorway to the bedroom, Father stood at the foot of the bed. Callie was bent over, rifling through a drawer. Father watched her in the mirror, admiring her cleavage. "I thought I had an extra towel in here," she said. As she slid the drawer closed, Callie turned around to face him. She tugged at the string of her dress. The dress fell open, revealing the tan of her stomach where I had seen her rub oil those mornings as she'd sunbathed on Otto's lawn. The thin string of her bikini was replaced by a sheer bra. Her crotch was barely covered by a small triangle of leopard print. Callie's form moved across the room toward Father as though in slow motion. With every step she seemed to become more feline and supple, dragging the paint of her toenails through the shag of the carpet. I waited for him to stop her.

When Callie was inches from Father's face, she stood with her feet shoulder width apart. She reached for his hand, moving it up to her shoulder, pausing for a moment to trace the outline of her breast. I watched as she slid the strap of her bra down the curve of her arm, the thick red of her nipple peering out from the cup as it fell. The rosacea on Father's forehead flared as it did under stress. Callie eased her way toward him and pushed him back onto the bed.

As their bodies met, the water bed gave way beneath them. The movement seemed to revive Father. He put one hand on Callie's chest and pushed her slightly away from him. With the other, he reached behind the small of his back. "There's something underneath us," he said. From behind his back Father produced a plastic action figure. The toy was missing a limb. Father held it in front of his face. "I told those boys not to play in my bed," Callie said. "No harm done," Father said placing the toy on the nightstand beside a bottle of antacids. Beside the bottle sat a book—*The Dance of Anger*—and an empty wine glass stained red at the bottom.

"I should go check on the chicken." Father said, and started to get up.

"Wait," Callie said.

I slipped away from the door and tiptoed down the hall.

The chicken was burnt and slightly charcoaled on one side.

"Something smells mighty good in here," I heard Father say as he came up behind me. He put his arm around my shoulder to steady himself. "Good girl, Jeannie," he said. "I can always count on you to take up the slack in a pinch."

As Callie came into the kitchen, he stiffened. "Let me set the table," he said picking up a stack of plates from the counter. Callie reached for her Marlboro Reds where she'd left them next to the chopping board. She picked up the pack and flicked the top of her nail several times against the bottom as though settling something. "It's your call," she said.

Father disappeared into the dining room and Callie turned toward the stove. "Dinner's on," she yelled to her boys out the window. As Callie exhaled a long deep drag of smoke, Birdie let go of the hoop where she hung. Rod caught her, cradling Birdie in his arms as he walked toward the house. In the light of the court, the two looked triumphant. Birdie's blonde ringlets spread out over Rod's shoulder. Her hair gleamed against the flannel of his shirt.

"Who's ready for some bird?" Father said as Rod and the boys came into the kitchen.

We ate in the dining room, a small square set of oak furniture erected in an alcove off the kitchen. The walls were papered in a faded pink floral. The floor was a worn orange shag. Save the vintage chandelier Callie had hung over the table, the room had the feel of having once been something else. A nursery perhaps.

"Yes to everything," Father was saying, "That's the problem with kids these days. They've never been told no." Father was telling Rod about his trials with the Steelhead brothers. Lately they'd been calling the house at night and hanging up the phone. Liden was onto Fender and I about the magazines.

"Boys will be boys," Rod said. "If you burn too much of your fist into them, they turn into a pack of wailing sissies. And there's nothing I hate more than a sissy."

"Right," Father said crossing and uncrossing his legs. "Well I suppose it's different. I'm surrounded by a house full of girls."

"Lucky man," Rod said, smiling at Father. "I suppose there's always room for another in the mix. Isn't that what you're up to here?"

"You're insufferable," Callie said to her husband under her breath. She looked proud of herself. Her cheeks flared under the bone.

"When's the last time someone said no to you Rick?" Rod said to Father.

After dinner we all went out into the yard to feed the yearling. The cow was waiting for us at the gate near the shed. They'd set him loose in a small run they'd patched together out of an old white slat-board fence and sections of chicken wire.

"Sturdy little fellow," Father said, holding Birdie up over the fence so she could reach the cow.

"The way that thing is growing, we should have steaks by fall," Rod said.

On the way home Father was silent.

"He used to be a wrestler," I said after a while. We were sailing down the hill on Merriam past the farmhouses in the center of town.

"Reach into the glove compartment," Father said. "Give me one of those cigars." He didn't hesitate to light one as he drove.

When we got back to the house Father settled into the couch in front of the news. "I'm going over to Otto's to check on the Sheik," I said.

"What time is it?" Father said looking out Mother's windows at the amount of light left in the sky. "Alright, so long as Otto's in the barn mucking the stalls. Be back before bed. And take the flashlight with you so I can watch out the window when you cross the road."

Light blasted through the windows that lined the front of Otto's barn as I ran across the street. It reminded me of an old movie theater, each stall screening a different run. I hurtled toward it, flashing the light once behind me so Father could see.

Wilson was raking the hay out of the aisle when I came in.

"Hi Wilson," I said. "It's just me. It's just Jean." Wilson looked up and focused on me for a minute.

"I went to camp today," he said. The way he was standing, belly over the belt, his chest puffed out, I could tell that today was a proud day for Wilson. It was odd to see an old man look so young again. He was bald and fat and graying. No less than forty in the light, the way the shadows clung to his face. And yet standing there in the aisle in that moment, his cheeks looked like a six year old's the first time he hits his first solid ball over the diamond. A good wind comes in from the outfield and brings some color into his face.

"Was she pretty?" I said.

"Yes," he said. "Daddy's proud of me. I went to camp and I met a redhead. A pretty girl."

"Your Daddy's always proud," I said.

"You're pretty too, Jeannie," he said. "Daddy says I like the pretty girls."

"There's few things I'm less wrong about than women," Otto said. I hadn't seen Otto standing at the far end of the barn. He must've been in the tack room settling the evening's chores when I'd come in. I knew he'd go there occasionally when the feed was on and the horses were settled for the night. I'd walked in on him one evening sitting at the draftsman desk he'd bought for His Helene back in the days when she still kept the books for the riding lessons they ran out of the barn.

Otto's face that night had a drawn, wan look that accompanies sleeplessness. I went to him out of pity.

"Tell the story again, old boy," he said to Wilson as I snuck up under Otto's armpit, wrapping one arm around his waist.

"What story?" Wilson said.

"The one about getting chased," Otto said, draping his arm over my shoulder. His body was fit for a man of his age. It had that taut tension that comes from the small inhalation of a parent thrilling over an act of their child's bravery.

"I went to visit the redhead in her cabin today," Wilson said.

"And who caught you, son?" Otto said, egging him on.

"The counselor," Wilson said. "He chased me out with a broom."

"And what did you tell him when he chased you?"

"I told him my Daddy said I like the pretty girls."

"That a way, son," Otto said. "You old bastard, you. You're just like your old man."

I looked up at Otto's eyes. A pride was rising in them, a glory he'd once thought fondly of and now recalled.

"That was a good one," Wilson said.

"It sure was," Otto said. "I'm proud of you. You might be ugly as shit but at least you're still chasing tail."

The two were laughing then. There was something in the way Otto laughed, his body doubled over, leaning forward toward his son standing in the thin light down the aisle, that made me realize that this was a feeling Otto'd been deprived of for a long while, the ability to connect with his son as a man. Otto glimpsed that for a moment. It felt damn good. They both felt damn good.

"The counselor said he thought he wanted to rape her," Otto said between breaths. He was laughing so hard he was almost sobbing. "I got a call this morning. Can you imagine? That dim wit actually thought my son had enough man in him to rape that girl."

Wilson understood his father's laugh as a sign of encouragement.

"Rake a girl," he said. "My Daddy says I'm gonna rake a girl."

Wilson took the rake in his arms and started spinning with it. He looked as if someone had dropped a harness around his belly, lifting him up toward the rafters, lending him grace and spin.

"Maybe I'll rake you, Jeanie," he said. "You're a pretty girl too."

Otto was chuckling all the way to the house. His arm was heavy on my shoulder as we walked. After all that, he seemed to have given up on something of the evening. I looked at the stars over top of us and thought of Wilson dancing and the sight of the power lines over Bluecreek. I thought about asking Otto what Wilson had meant by all that in the barn.

"Back to work now, son," he'd eventually said to Wilson when he got the air back in his chest. "That's enough of that."

"Will you be alright then?" I said to Otto.

"Right as rain," Otto said. "Why don't you come in for a minute and see if you can make that old piano play again."

The piano was a small upright Otto kept in the back room near the porch. The top of it resembled a bench from an earlier time, a resting place where all the old faces still sat around and kept watch on the day. It was lined with frames and trinkets, relics of the days when His Helene had still been working her hand and saying her say over her two boys. The collection had the feel of an album—all the best moments splayed together despite the shit faces and gap teeth.

I started in on a sonata, quietly and without much breath at first. But then with more confidence as I went. There was a seriousness about Otto which I respected. His was not a soul easily turned.

I looked over my shoulder at one point while I played. Otto was sitting in the recliner. A peacefulness had invaded his face.

I hadn't seen His Helene in the other room watching. She was sitting in her wheelchair with her feet in a bedpan. Here you are, she seemed to say, a bit of my letting go.

There I was, all these trinkets of hers, and her husband's eyes boring into me. By the time I got to the final movement I felt I knew something of her inner life. I tried to tell it just as I heard it. Strong faithful chords. Easy on the flutes and the runs. I wanted to splay the notes in good conscience.

"You've been lonely then too," His Helene said from the other room, when I had finished.

I went to her, kneeling down at her feet and putting my arms on her legs. I tried to be rough with her when I could to remind her that she was still a woman.

"Do you want to go for a stroll, Helene?" I said.

"Sure do, darlin'," she said. "It's frightful small in here tonight."

We bundled her in the old fur from the front closet and all of Otto's gear, her throat every bit covered. On her head we put the coon hat Otto wore riding in the winter. Wilson donated his glasses to shield her eyes. "We can't let the wind take those now can we," Otto said affixing them to her face. "There's no natural tears left."

It was true. I'd put the drops in. What water His Helene had left in her had congregated in her feet. They were bulbous and bloated. The doctor said next it would move to her heart. That's what would take her. That one big rush of her own stream.

She took her grapes. I put them in a small blue bowl, which I wedged on her lap. In a panic, she liked to feel a frozen grape on her tongue. The nurse had shown me where to place it.

Otto took the flashlight. Together we rolled His Helene into the night. Otto'd built a ramp off the back porch that she'd used to wheel herself out to the barn when she'd still had some strength in her arms.

"Take her around front," Otto said. "I want to show her off one last time even if there's no one to see her."

It took too much emotion out of him to push. He just wanted to run alongside and watch the fear being lifted from her face. I broke into a steady jog after we cleared the driveway. The shadows of the branches overhead splayed out on her lap. I watched them move over her as we ran.

"Go, go, go," she said.

After a few laps, Otto sat on the porch and held the light for us. We made a few more runs in front of the house. I wondered if Father was watching as we passed. I wondered if someday I wouldn't be doing this with him too.

When I feared the cold would take her, I took her in. As I undressed her, His Helene started to panic. She could feel the gravity shifting. The water in her feet had begun its migration.

Otto went for her box of shots in the freezer. Some high-altitude sedative. That kind of devil had to be kept fresh. Once the needle was under the skin, His Helene looked peaceful. We laid her out on the pullout in the front room. She slept on the ground floor of the house. Otto feared she'd fall down the stairs. The other night, he'd said, she had managed to push herself out of bed and had taken a few steps before crashing into the bookcase. He'd found her on the floor struggling to lift her face out of the carpet. She'd fought him off kicking and wailing.

"You'll suffocate yourself," he'd said.

"Who says I'll let you kill me like this," she'd replied.

Otto wouldn't get a night nurse. He said people wait for everyone to leave a room before they die. "Sometimes," he said, "I pace the house just to give her room to slip away."

Once His Helene was quiet we went out onto the front porch to get some air. Outside there was a weightiness between us. I stood next to Otto on the mat that lined the door looking out at the road.

"What do you do," he said, "when there's almost no one left?"

The way he took me in his arms, pulling the small of my waist into his belt, I felt the sudden surging up of all the ways I'd wanted to be needed. I saw Mother in Father's arms that morning as they'd danced next to the drain board in the kitchen. I saw Callie push Father into her bed. And too, I saw everything of His Helene. I tilted my head back. He was careful with my lips.

Afterward, Otto took my face in his hands and turned it sideways examining my profile under the gloomy spin of the porch light. There was a softness to my chin which the dentist had once suggested doing away with. "A little insert," he'd said, turning my face in his hand just as Otto did now, showing Father my weakness in the mirror of the examination room. "Best to correct for any overbite before she grinds her teeth and lockjaw sets in."

"You have a long nose," Otto said.

"It belongs to my mother," I said.

"It's good to know what belongs where," he said.

It was late. Or it was getting late. But there was something in the way Otto looked at me, that pride brimming up in his eyes, I was afraid to leave it alone. "Come inside," he said. "I'll put us on a pot of coffee and some cards."

"I suppose I could deal just one hand," I said.

The table in the kitchen was littered with piles of hospital bills, dirty coffee cups, and mountains of discarded creamers.

We sat across from each other. The table was small. Our knees touched from time to time.

"He doesn't mean any harm," Otto said nodding toward the RV where Wilson had retired as he poured a glass of Whiskey. "He's just looking for someone his own age. There isn't anyone left."

"Who's left for you?" I said.

"Well," he said. "Callie keeps me busy from time to time."

"How long have you known her?" I said.

"Long enough," he said. "To hate her a little. I've raised her like one of my own."

"I've seen her on your lawn," I said.

"Always up and out the door before the next day breaks over top of her," he said. "Never could shake the life out."

He reached out across the table and handed me the cards. The box was soft and worn at the edges.

"Deal me a good hand, Jeanie," he said, taking my hands in his as I reached for the deck. A wind came in through the slat where the window next to the table was open. The old hobbyhorse clanged against the side of the house in the breeze. I could make out the outline of its hooves where they hung in the dim light of the porch, the thin strips of gun-metal silver. I wondered how old Callie had been when she'd spray-painted her name on its rump and where she'd ridden it on his lawn.

"I'll deal," I said. "You cut the deck."

There's something about hands that cuts to the quick of a man. Otto's were lithe and narrow, with large boxish fingernails which he kept clipped close to the flesh. Watching them move over the pile of cards reminded me of the way Grandfather had once sharpened knives in a steady arc against the carving stone in his kitchen. "A fast even clip," Grandfather had said. "That's where you find your edge." Otto's hands flipped and spit with the same confidence. Here was a man without patience for clumsiness or idle. He'd had so much backward speed fall into his life, it was all he could do to get himself and his son washed each morning. Every now and again he groomed his own mustache or changed the straight pin on his lapel. Occasionally, when he needed to get away from the world, he cracked his whip at the air for a while.

Otto flipped his last card. I still had two on deck.

"I win," Otto said.

"You always win," I said.

The speed fell out of us. At some hour Otto's Scotch turned into Whiskey. My cup he filled with sweet cognac, which he cut with a teaspoon of sugar. The edges of the cards adopted a haze. Each time Otto shuffled they fluttered momentarily.

His knees gripped mine.

I got up to go the bathroom. How long I sat on that yellow toilet seat counting the cracks in the rim, I couldn't say. When I came out, the room was spinning and my body had taken on a leftward lilt. I stood for a moment in the hallway and steadied myself against the expanse of wall. Otto was in the living room with his tumbler of Scotch regarding the pale screen of the television, its lead-bellied glow illuminating the thick grain of the carpet, which he hadn't bothered to vacuum since His Helene had stopped entertaining and now lent considerable dirt to the bottom of the foot. Skeeter Davis's "The End of the World" played on the hi-fi. Otto wore his field boots inside the house as of late. He said he feared gnats. He feared lice. He feared paper fleas on account of the newspapers he kept stored in the wood crate next to the fireplace. Some nights, he said, he awoke to the feeling that a strange mold was growing up his throat on account of the floorboards. The earth around the foundation had crumbled in recent years. In the winter when the snow came in under the house, the floors were damp for weeks. He'd taken to packing old trash bags with dried leaves to try and patch up the gullys under the house where he could. The bags provided little protection. When the wind got to raging he swore he could hear it cursing the floor beneath him.

Other nights, he'd told me, he woke to the feeling that the house had been raised off the earth. I imagined him in his robe throwing himself toward the window in order to look out and regain some sense of his habitation. There was the earth. There was the barn. He searched for the line of trees in the distance to convince himself the house itself hadn't been swept from the earth like some dwelling in the Malaysian peninsula which stood suspended next to the shore on thin legs of reed in case the river swelled after the storm. A kelong they called it. He'd seen the word in a recurring dream.

The dream, as he'd told it, began with a knock at the door. His first thought was of his wife. He was living in a motel next to the sea in the old fishing town in Galicia where he'd gone to dry out his head after the war. His Helene had caught him at the door with a towel around his waist, some dark-eyed woman who he'd met behind the glass at the currency exchange laying in the blue glare of the rented bed.

His second thought was that the police were on to him. When he opened the door, a man who looked like Wilson handed him a summons. "D. B. Cooper?" Wilson said. "You signed a bad check to the bank." In 1971 D. B. Cooper had boarded a Boeing 727 on flight between Oregon and Washington, ordered a drink and announced to the stewardess that he had a bomb in his bag. After receiving a sack-full of ransom at a refueling in Reno, D. B. Cooper ordered the plane disembark and fly south to Mexico. He'd plummeted mid-flight with the money.

Alone under the weight of his anxieties, the dream, Otto'd said, took on the presence of his reality. Cooper was a man of sophistication and precision. After announcing to the stewardess that he had a bomb, he'd ordered a bourbon and water, paid his tab, and told the stewardess to keep the change. "Looks like Tacoma down there," he'd said reassuringly. Of D. B. Cooper's effects two items stood out in Otto's mind, his black attaché case and his mother-of-pearl tiepin. Otto himself owned a mother of pearl pin, which his wife had given him when their first horse had won the Grand Prix.

As I walked into the living room, the newscaster on the television was talking about a euthanasia machine. The image of a woman who looked not unlike Mother flashed across the scene. "And this stops the heart as soon as it reaches it," a thin elderly doctor named Kevorkian said leaning over a machine which resembled His Helene's series of drip tubes hanging next to the pullout in the corner where she now lay. "Her decision had been made some time ago," the husband of the woman on the television said. The image of the crummy old van in an RV park where Kevorkian had attached the woman to her death looked almost identical to the RV in back of Otto's house where Wilson now slept. I looked at the woman's face on the screen and looked over at His Helene on the pullout. Helene's thin, colorless head was propped up on a pillow, a few wisps of hair brushed over her temple. It was hard to tell if she was watching.

Otto slumped over on the couch in front of the window. The shades behind him were cracked open just enough that I could see the outline of the Bottom Feeder in the background, Father and Birdie asleep in it, wallowing in the shadows across the street. Slowly I approached the old man. "Shoeless," I reassured Otto, taking his worn-out body into my arms on the sofa as he fumbled to get my dress over my head. "It's like boarding a train, I promise."

"Just lie back," I said.

Or, maybe he said, "Just look out the window."

Have you ever seen Skeeter Davis sing "The End Of the World"? Really seen it? "Hey, listen. Why don't we have Skeeter Davis do another song right now," the host of the night show says. And this angelic platinum haired woman who looks not unlike Birdie stands in front of the microphone in a dress buttoned up to her chin and sings, "Why does the sun keep on shining? Why does the sea rush to shore? Don't they know it's the end of the world cause you don't love me anymore?"

This is what I pictured as Otto pulled my dress over my head that night. Birdie as Skeeter Davis performing at a carnival on television, her blonde hair aglow and the world watching. I imagined the scout who had stopped Mother in the mall and looked at Birdie and said, "Hey, that kid would show up well on television." And I thought of my ugly little chin and the dentist's stale breath in my face as he'd whispered, "Just a little insert." And the way Father wanted to keep his girls a little ugly, the better to protect our brains.

The old man began to kiss my neck and reach for his belt beneath me. I stopped him. "Let me do it," I said. I undressed him the way Mother had done for Father, the way Birdie and I had practiced. His body was boxy and not unathletic. The way his skin hung loose over the bones you could tell he'd left something of himself behind. He'd let something get away from him, love or lust or maybe just time. In the process, he'd gotten smaller.

He held my head into his neck. He didn't want me to see him. I remember the pain pushing up into me little by little and then more forcefully until he could no longer manage. The pain, the shock of it, provided an opening, into which I could recede. I came to understand what to do, there was a steady rhythm to it.

"You can look at me and say, 'You're a criminal,'" Kevorkian said on the television.

It was Wilson who interrupted us. He was standing at the window. His breath fogged a halo around his face in the glass. When I looked up, he waved.

"Don't encourage him," Otto said without turning his head.

"Who's encouraging who?" I said.

"He's better off outside," Otto said.

"I'll check on him," I said.

"Let him watch," he said. "That yard's not big enough for an old hound dog to scare up a squirrel. I should worry. It's not often I get a woman like you in my lap."

I straightened my spine. Every now and again Wilson moved his palm against the glass to clear the fog. I had all the attention he'd ever wanted.

How it ended I don't remember. The room had taken on a slant by the time the dog started barking.

"Do me a favor, Jeanie," Otto said, my clothes strewn across the floor. "Let that mutt out to do his business."

I stood and walked across the living room carpet and onto the cool slip of kitchen linoleum in my bare feet with my flat chest shining. The minute I opened the back door, I smelled Wilson's stench. A pool of urine had gathered at his feet where he'd been watching. As the old Setter ran outside, he leapt over the standing liquid. Wilson looked down at the dark trail that stained the front of his pants and laughed. Tears were coming down his cheeks.

"Pretty girl, Jeanie," he said. "Daddy says I like the pretty girls."

Otto was on him before I heard the crash of the chair in the kitchen behind me from where Otto'd overturned it. I felt the rush of the old man's body and the stale whiff of Scotch as he sailed through the doorway. His hand landed solidly against Wilson's face. The crack of skin against skin was sharp and high. At the last minute Otto released his fist. At least his palm was open. The way the shadows caught Wilson's features, all I saw was the slack skin of his jaw and the long wrinkled gullet under his chin flap sideways from the impact.

In that moment, I knew Otto Houser was a spy. He was trading for some old team where he'd once had a bit part as a pitch hitter. All that slapping and shouting. When he looked at me he saw a way back into those days when he'd spun his wife around the old inn in Cheshire where they were married among the silver and the paintings of hunting dogs and cavalry that hung on the porch. After the war and the bum kid and the thing cleaved inside of His Helene's lungs, he'd dragged himself back to that place on his belly. He'd righted himself on the portico of that old inn with a bottle of whiskey and an envelope of lists. Everyone on Fay Mountain could see the way he clung there to the banister. His cheeks had sallowed. Only the liquor brought back the rush of light to his eyes. He had his felt derby hat and his long tan cigarettes that left the yellow around his gums and under his nails. People still envied him for his head of hair. Everything else he had was built on nostalgia. That brown and white Spaniel at his chair under the table could just as soon have been the reincarnation of some old porcelain figurine cutting up a rust on top of the piano had it not been for the way he licked his master's feet.

I grabbed my dress from the floor and took off across the yard before I saw the look in Wilson's eyes. I was afraid they would still be laughing.

As I crossed the road that separated our houses, I heard a long deep wailing followed by the yapping of a dog. I stopped in the shadows beneath the two trees of knowledge, and slid my underwear from around my waist. A stain had gathered on the moist strip of white cotton where it had clung between my legs. I held it up to the moon to examine it. In the crotch there was thin streak of blood. I buried the underwear between two rocks in the stone wall. The lights in Otto Houser's house were off by the time I entered the Bottom Feeder and locked the door behind me.

Father was asleep in the recliner in front of the television. The war was still going on.

16.

The next morning the rain came. One of those warm summer downpours that follows the opening up of the sky and a great movement of air.

There was a note from Father in the kitchen. "Went riding with Otto." K was sitting at the table with a mug of coffee. Even her skin looked pale and gray in this light. "He didn't want to wake you," she said. As I reached for the door of the refrigerator, I felt a presence occupy my body, as though I were outside myself watching the morning break over us. K, or the semblance of K, returned to thumbing one of the women's magazines Mother had delivered to the house.

It wasn't unlike Father to set out at that hour. He was often at his best in the morning when the sun had released him from the confinement of his bed.

I poured two tall glasses of juice. K and I stumbled into the living room and the drone of the television. K was lax to settle on any one program. The images on the screen barely registered. I just needed some buzzing between us.

The phone was ringing after a while too.

It was a woman. It was Mother. Or it sounded like Mother would sound if she was shouting across some long field.

"Is that you, Jeanie?" she said. "Do you still have that same twang in your voice? Is that how you sound?"

"It's still me, Mom," I said, unsure of the answer myself as I was saying it.

"Oh," she said.

"What?" I said.

"Nothing," she said. "I'm just a little nervous."

"Why?" I said.

"Nothing," she said. "I'm always a little nervous in the afternoons."

"Oh," I said, pausing for a moment to scan the mist in the field visible through the window over the sink. The world outside looked not unlike one of Father's Bob Ross imitations, faint and hazy around the edges. The tree line barely etched in with his chisel. "It's still morning here."

"Anyways," Mother said. "Your grandmother just burnt her pie."

There was a pause then. I could hear the air rushing over the receiver. It sounded as if Mother were shouting in a vacuum, a long narrow tube laid next to a highway. Occasionally, a car whooshed by.

"It's still morning here too," she said.

She'd run to Granny Olga's old gaping house. There was enough space there for getting lost. There, she fostered what the children of all first generation immigrants feared, an innate feeling that the day to day was long and hard and struggling but as the city teamed around you progress was being made. The struggle was the pride of it. It was only in the face of adversity that Mother was ever truly free. Under Mother's feet, there was the kind of ice made for skating. It was thin. But she was light.

"Where's that?" I said. "Where you are."

"Here," she said. "Outside of the Stewarts."

We'd used the pay phone there together once when we'd forgotten a carton of cream that Granny Olga had wanted. Or a certain spice. We'd rung her up with a dime Mother had found wedged between the seats of the Toyota. "White pepper," Granny Olga had said. "Creamed corn." "Remember that," Mother had said as she went back into the store. "Or she'll have our heads, the both of us."

"I hope I didn't wake you," Mother said.

"No," I said. "You didn't. I just got up."

"Well fine," she said. "Is your father around?"

"He's out," I said. "He went riding with Otto." I paused, trying to steady my breath.

"Well that's fine then too," Mother said. "Some things are as they are."

"Sure," I said.

"Well," she said. "Look after your sister."

"I will, Mom," I said.

"Good," she said. "Oh, and Jean. Look after yourself a little too."

"Sure," I said.

"Is there anyone there with you?" she said. "Or did he leave you two to your own devices? I hate thinking of you two left to your own devices."

"K's here," I said, looking into the living room at the dough-faced girl lolling on our couch.

"Is that her name?" she said. "I thought it was Kat or Katherine. Yes, it was Katherine. I remember meeting her once and thinking she looked like Catherine Deneuve."

"Maybe it is," I said, examining the girl's face more closely as she tapped her cigarette out the window and yawned.

"I've been mistaken for a Katherine you know," Mother said. "People used to say I looked like an actress. I could've been in films."

"I know," I said. "I remember."

"I know you know," she said laughing a little. "Does it scare you that your old Mom was once mistaken for someone other than who she is?"

I didn't know who Catherine Deneuve was. I looked in at K, or Kat, or Katherine, the small pudgy-faced girl stomaching around on our couch with her legs stretched skyward. I imagined her as she would look as a Catherine. Her hair done up in a wave that gave several inches of rise to her face and highlighted her cheekbones making her look finer than she was.

I could imagine someone mistaking Mother that way.

"No," I said. "I'm not scared."

"Good," Mother said. "That was all some time ago anyways. Now I'm your mother. You know me as your mother. I still want you to think of me that way."

"Sure," I said.

"Well," she said.

Her voice dropped out after that. I had the feeling that the line had died. There was the static. And the distance. And the Stewarts. Mother was saying something about K again.

"Is she often over?" she said.

"Not too often," I said.

"Well," she said. "I meant to talk to you about that before I left. I meant to talk to you about men and their ideas."

"OK," I said.

"I don't know if you know what I mean yet," she said. "But one day you will and we will talk about it."

"Right," I said.

"Well good," she said. "Then one day soon we'll talk about it. In the meantime, keep an eye out for me."

"Sure, Mom," I said.

"I don't know what's going on over there, but you know what I mean about your father and that girl."

"Callie?" I said.

"No," she said. "Katherine. Or whatever girl he's hired to replace me. Don't let her get her claws into him. And call me if she does."

It was hard to imagine the plump teen lounging on the settee next to the window raising her claws to a man. All K dragged out of the world was a relief from momentary inertia. Even when her boyfriend stopped by, when she rose up into him in the doorway and kissed him on the mouth, the most she drew out of him was the faint stench of sweat. Afterwards, she released the smell out the window and was back to her smokes.

"OK," I said.

"Your father thinks he could do no wrong," Mother said. "The way you girls coddle him."

"He's my father," I said.

"Well sure," she said. "But he's a man too. And sometimes he's not half the man you've raised him up to be in reputation."

"Reputation?" I said.

"It just means keep your eyes out for your mother. And don't you go rising up into his arms too often either," she said. "He's lonely, you know. Yes. I imagine he's quite lonely there."

I could hear the skittishness coming back into her voice. She would hang up soon. Soon she would be on her way back to us.

"OK," I said.

I hung up the receiver. The refrigerator kicked in.

When I returned to the living room, K was painting her nails. She was sitting on the edge of the L-shape, one knee drawn up to her stomach, her foot poised on the edge of the cushion revealing a long line of toes, which she covered with a red gloss. I recognized the bottle. Mother kept it in the back of the drawer where she stashed the compacts she used to paint her face those nights she was going out. On K the polish looked thick and cheap. Something about the color made me want to vomit. The way she went down the row, her eyes barely moving from the screen of the television to dab or wipe a smudge, I doubt she cared much.

Birdie was curled up next to her. A box of cereal wedged between them. They were watching that program again about the circus pony who'd learned to dive.

"Go, go, go," Birdie said grabbing her feet and flinging them in the air.

"Easy there, Little Wonder," K said. "You'll upset my color."

I felt outside myself. I had not entirely left the void I'd entered the night before. Standing in the doorway watching K and Birdie's bodies across the room was like watching the exposed side of a mountain in a storm. The more the rain came on, the more their expressions washed into a sheen. Eventually their eyes eroded into shutters. The shutters flicked open from time to time revealing a faint light behind them. Probably just a reflection of the glare from the tube.

"Have a seat, soldier," K said to me, her eyes challenging mine for a moment. "You're making your sister nervous hovering like that."

"It's okay, Jean," Birdie eventually said. "It's just a movie.

"I know," I said.

I looked out the window behind them. Through the fog I could make out the bodies of The Sheik and Father's big Morgan. Their heads were down, grazing in the doctor's field. The brown patches of their saddles rose and fell as they shuddered along looking for new spots of green. I'd seen horses graze so many times this way. The absence of any rider didn't strike me until I heard someone laying hard and long on the doorbell.

In the brightness of the morning light Otto's body looked pale and shrunken. I shuddered at the sagging chicken skin of his neck where he stood on the other side of the door. He was half way through the archway before I had the chance to shut him out.

"Get your mother on the phone," Otto said. His eyes were expressionless. "Tell her we're headed to the hospital. Tell her your father would like to see her there. Tell her I said so."

Father was sitting away from us at the far end of the narrow slab of concrete that served as our porch. After he saw me look at him, he put his head in his hands and walked off some distance toward the stream to hide the damage. His face had rearranged itself into a dark mass not so different from the field that had rearranged it that way.

As Otto later recalled the accident, he'd never seen an animal go down with so much weight. They'd been galloping, sure. But they hadn't been so crazy as to go open reigning in that weather. It was the fault of the rain and the slick of the mud, Otto said.

That and Father's big old Morgan had too much of the carriage in him. He was sturdy on his feet but undependable in the wet. His rear went out from under. Father went down with him. His foot had caught in the stirrup. There was nothing between Father's face and the corn. "I'll be damned about that rain," Otto joked with Father some days later. "It'll turn even the tiniest field into something famous."

"Next time," Father said, "I'll put some cleats on that fella."

"Sure," Otto said. "Or don't take a carriage horse out sledding in the rain."

A stalk had nearly pierced Father's eye. It had threaded itself in the soft spot next to the socket. One eyelid was hanging. Everything else was swollen shut save for the opposite side of his mouth. When he went to speak, he tongued the gap where his tooth was missing. The blood let down from his gums. "Take your sister and get back in the house," he said. "Everything's all right here. It's a close call is all."

I resisted making the call. Otto went inside to use the phone. When he came back he had a bag of ice in one hand and one of Father's flannels in the other. He wrapped the shirt around Father's head. The two men shouldered down the walk toward the Bronco where it was parked in the gravel next to the drive.

The Starlings' green truck crested the hill. Otto had put the call out to them too.

As the two cars passed on the road, Ray saluted Father through the windshield and swung into our driveway. He parked in the gravel next to the house and turned down the engine. Ruth took over the kitchen and put on a spread while Ray smoked his cigar on the porch. He was drunker than usual from the heat. His smell was thick. He moved as though swimming.

I sat in Father's rocking chair in the corner. Dumb. Silent. A witness to something but I wasn't sure what.

"I imagine you can go now," Ruth said peeking her head out from the oven and speaking to K. "There's no need for more bodies in this house."

"If you think so," K said.

"Sure," Ruth said. "Just let Ray know you mean to be going. He'll drive you home." Ruth was in her element. The pressure of an emergency was thrilling. Within the hour eggs and pancakes and the half-box of Entenmann's, which she'd grabbed from her counter and stuffed in her purse, appeared on our table. Afterwards, she turned the light off and made a pot of coffee for her and Ray. The dishes she hand washed in the half-light and stacked on a yellow hand rag. The dishwasher brought too much heat into the house. When she was done, she sat with us and watched the night shows that ran in the weekend slot after the morning cartoons, fifties sitcoms, old black and whites with the laugh tracks. Ruth's laugh was easy and inviting. Anyone would've chuckled along with her under different circumstance. That afternoon as the sound of her voice reverberated off the thin walls, I wondered if it wouldn't finally blow out Mother's windows altogether and let the world in to consume us.

The day passed by way of the rain. First sheeting and then intermittent waves of mist that descended and ascended in a rolling pattern as dry patches of air moved into the swamplands absorbing some of the moisture until the drizzle came and the doctor's fields were saturated again. Despite the heat and the film on her face, Ruth kept us in meals. Every few hours she went into the kitchen to prepare something, which occasionally one of us picked at until the temperature got the best of it and she plated whatever it was and put it in the fridge to keep. Ray returned from dropping K home. I showed him where Mother kept the jug of cooking rum. He went outside with the bottle and swept the porch for a while.

It was dark by the time Father's Bronco rolled into the drive. Otto was at the wheel, Father alongside him. Time resumed with the slam of a car door and the sound of the two men making their way up the gravel. A second pair of headlights soon fronted the street. I could make out Granny Olga's hair as the car turned into the drive. Gramps's white Panama hat still shone from where she kept it on the ledge in the rear of the Buick.

"Lord, child," Granny Olga said clutching the hem of my dress before her bags were through the door. "Get yourself upstairs and put on something decent."

The moment Mother entered the house every switch was tossed. The lights were on and the windows were open. She was sharing a cigarette with Otto who had her on one arm and her bags on the other. Father was in an unusually light mood. Despite the fact that his face had been beaten and bruised, he was quick on his feet. He was joking about the hard time the hospital had given them. "Nurses. Stiff upper lip from the start. Swore I'd been in a bar fight," Father was recounting to Ray. "They were jealous of my wife's right hook."

"That's not all they were jealous of," Otto egged him on. Otto's flattery went a long way in reviving them. Even Granny Olga gave up a tight-wadded snicker.

Ruth was in kitchen again with the eggs and the éclairs. What with the emergency, we'd worked up an appetite. Granny Olga was bothering Ruth about the tea. There was nothing like a good Catholic woman in her daughter's kitchen to stir up Granny Olga's hankering to bring out the samovar. Once, I'd asked Mother about attending catechism.

"I want to go," I'd said. I'd just finished sitting down to my method. Mother had come into the room to have a cigarette and a listen. It was the only time Mother had ever struck me in the face. The surprise of it was what stung.

Despite her husband's alcoholism and her penchant for Pall Malls, Ruth was a Catholic. Grandmother could smell it on her, lapsed or no.

"I'll clean up here, darlin'," Granny Olga said as soon as Ruth had finished arranging her spread.

The house had the feel of the holidays.

"I heard Jean's been tending to Helene," Mother was saying to Otto. Everyone was sprawled out on the L-shape.

"With all her grace," Otto said. "Never thought I'd see anyone make that old piano sing again," he said.

"I keep telling her," Father said. "She could really have something if she just practiced. Not everyone can have a little something like that. A real talent."

"I think she practices just fine," Otto said.

I was quiet then. My eyes fell into my lap. I examined the curve of my thigh where Grandmother had touched it. I thought maybe I'd have a fine shape one day if I just discovered it right.

"Speak up, child," Granny Olga said. "We don't mind you so much talking."

Otto cleared his throat. He began telling stories about the bonfire.

"All this celebrating in my absence," Mother was saying. "You know how much I hate to miss a good party."

"Nothing doing," Father said. "Pretty much just a fire and some fancy camping is all. Remember, baby. I took you camping once."

"Sure," Mother said. She hadn't given in to him yet. But she wasn't denying him anything either. He was injured after all. Everyone could see that. Everyone could see that denying him would've made her look too sharp in the light.

"We ate fresh carp," she said.

"Crappie," Father said. "We went swimming and fried crappie over the Bunsen and camped out on the dock. We never made it all the way out to the ocean. You said you wanted to avoid the salt."

"Right," Mother said. "I never can get the water out of my eyes. That was it."

"I don't know what you kids call camping," Otto said. "All I know is I came home from the butte that night with a six pack under one arm and a hard-on under the other despite the liquor. I haven't been that horny since I was a teen. I went to take a piss and caught myself in the zipper. Wilson comes in and I'm curled up on the floor with my head over the bowl. Scared him shitless. All that smoke and wide open air."

"Cocksucker," Ray said then from the rocker. It was hard to say if this was intended as a comment on the conversation or if it was just some gesticulation.

"Get back to your sleep, old man," Otto said.

"Well," Father said to Otto. "I guess I'll have to button you up better next time. I took you for a man who could hold his liquor."

"That's what being out in the daybreak will do to you," Mother said, pausing for a moment to stare at Father. "It messes with your sense of the day."

"Sure," Otto said. "The sunrise spoils everything."

They both laughed. They both seemed easier then.

"Speaking of fresh air," Granny Olga said and nodded down at me. She was talking about my age and the conversation. She'd given up trying to get me to dress. She was on to smoothing my hair.

"There's no use waterproofing her," Mother said, nodding towards me. "She's got a good mind. A little love and squalor isn't gonna change that. A little love and squalor isn't going to change anything."

There was a knock at the front door.

"Be a doll and get that," Mother said to me. She tapped me on the bottom as she excused me from the room. One day her daughter might have a figure too if she just gave it the right attention.

Callie had come to visit the scene of Mother's crime. All Callie's desires had been laid there in our house in Mother's absence. Callie glanced into the living room through the open door. She looked tired. Her breathing was heavy. Her hair smelled of ointment.

"I heard from the barn hand," she said. "The horses came home without any riders. I saw him leading them in."

"How are they?" I said.

"Who?" she said.

"The horses," I said.

"Fine," she said. "The horses are fine. The vet's there now."

"Thanks for staying with them," I said.

"Sure," she said.

"Sorry," I said.

"Sorry for what?" she said.

"That you've put so much into looking after them."

She was gazing at the eagle, the small one in the painting over the wooden chest where I kept my sleeping bag for those mornings I waited on the Steelhead mother's Impala.

"Where'd she pick that up?" Callie said nodding toward the painting.

"Junk shop," I said.

"Ah," she said. "I thought maybe it meant something. I thought maybe he'd painted it for her."

"Who?" I said.

"No one," she said. "Your old man." I knew then how much Callie'd thought on Father. How much of herself she'd wasted away hoping. Like most things that were sinking, she'd seen something shift here and had hoped to grab hold of it. I looked in at Father. His face was puffy and blue. He was smiling with all the teeth he had. I could tell by the way he ignored the door, that Callie was a thought that had not yet occurred to him. Her image was still stuck there developing somewhere in the ether. He was a good man. All he'd wanted to do was fix her pipes.

"Oh," I said. "Father doesn't paint much anymore."

Callie took my chin briefly in her hand and tilted it toward her face so that she could shove her smile into my eyes. I swallowed that too.

"You look like her," she said.

"Who?" I said.

"Your mother," she said. "She's nearly glowing."

"Yes," I said. "Mother's quite well."

Callie looked at me then with a new sort of terror. There was something welling up in her eyes. It looked almost like laughter. "Happy to hear it," she said. "I'm sure she's happy to see you."

"I suppose," I said. "It's been a long day. She's been traveling."

"Well," she said, "Tell Otto His Helene's been asking for him. Tell him I put a pot of coffee on."

"Is she in a bad way?" I said.

"Yes," she said. "I suppose she is in a bad way."

"Sure," I said. "I'll tell him."

"Well," she said. "I best be getting home."

"Are you sure?" I said, opening the door a little further to let her have one last look at them.

"I'm sure," she said. "I have my boys."

"Who was that?" Mother said when I came back to the couch.

"No one," I said. "The stable boy. He came to let us know about the horses."

"How are they?" she said.

"Who?" I said.

"The horses," she said.

"They're fine," I said. "He said the horses are fine."

Otto was the last out the door that night. He'd wanted to make his presence felt. He'd roll up his sleeves. He'd helped with the dishes. He'd even taken Granny Olga for a little turn in the kitchen.

"The key is to let the cat out the bag and be done with it," I overheard Otto saying to Father as Father turned down the lights and showed the old man out.

It was late by the time Mother appeared in the doorway to my little room. I'd taken my time getting ready. I didn't want to appear as though I was waiting. We'd gotten along well enough on our own.

There was something deflated about Mother that evening. The way she leaned against the doorframe for a moment peering

122

in at me, I could tell she wanted to feel something. I wanted to feel it too.

"Come in the bathroom for a minute," she said. "I want to show you what I found."

The tile under my feet was firm and reassuring. The night cast around what little courage it could. I could tell from Mother's stance that this was a speaking opportunity. She wanted to impart something that only she could demonstrate.

"Is it yours?" she said leaning over the plastic wastebasket next to the toilet.

The basket was thick with paper. On top of the mountain of white there was a sanitary napkin. K's I supposed.

"No," I said. "I haven't gotten it yet." There was a pause then as we both stared down at the thin strip of blood barely visible in the light. I thought of the underwear I'd buried between the rocks in the stone wall under the trees of knowledge.

I looked at Mother's face over the toilet in the dim light searching for some signal of recognition. All I saw was a tiny barefoot woman with a far off scare in her eye. Her chest was thin and hollow. For some reason I felt like crying. I had disappointed her, not because of what I had done but because I was still a child hanging on her belt who hadn't grown up and out yet.

"Good girl," Mother said again. "That's all right then."

A rush of shaking and tears started quietly and then lit into me all at once. I couldn't get the air in. This was all the reason Mother needed. She took me into her arms.

"It'll come," she said pulling me close to her.

"Anyways," she said, "Any half decent woman would know enough to bury it a little under the paper."

When I was sure the house was good and quiet, I made my way downstairs. Granny Olga was sleeping in the room next to the laundry in the basement. Her door was open a crack. Her snoring was regular. The hall smelled of Vicks and patchouli.

The door to the crawlspace was the only one that didn't squeak. I closed it quietly behind me, putting a shoe between the door and the frame so I could get in again if I needed.

Outside it was cool. I sat on the rock under the apple tree. The damp had set in. I felt smaller than I expected. It was a relief. The road was there if I needed somewhere to run.

When I got cold enough, I wandered over to Father's Bronco. The front seat was a banquette. I lay down on it. With the windshield above me, I still had the stars. The sun would be in my eyes before the next day had broken. I'd be up by the time Callie appeared on Otto's lawn, before they knew I'd gone missing.

For now, it was enough to sleep out.

17.

I was awoken by the sun. My body must have moved some in sleep. The back of Father's T-shirt, my usual sleeping gown, had climbed my torso in the night. It clung in a ball to the sweat at the small of my back. I looked down. My hip bones jutted out from the velour of the Bronco. I gripped the two bones where they rose up from my body as though they alone might direct the vehicle. There was a flatness to the stretch of stomach between them. I admired its shape. That small placid sea.

There was a certainty to the way the door of the Bronco closed behind me. The lock clicked into place and I started for the Bottom Feeder. As I walked up the stone path toward the porch I had the sensation of the road spiraling toward me as if I'd once again been dropped into a world that had receded from my grasp. Even the grass looked sharp and crisp and tangible. The gnarled stems of the apple trees whose heads had once appeared rabid with blossom now leaned out of the lawn no larger than two small shrubs. There was a tightness in my chest as I strode toward the Bottom Feeder that morning. It migrated down to my stomach and the small of my back which felt connected as if by a some small piece of string where Otto Hauser had held it.

Granny Olga was in the kitchen. Despite the bed of wild-flowers whose current drifted in through the windows, the house smelled of cabbage and onion.

"Morning, Gran," I said.

"Morning, child," she said. "You're up awful early."

"I forgot to pull the shades," I said.

"I told your mother she should install those curtains," she said.

"The shades work alright," I said. "As long as I don't forget to pull them. If I do, the day breaks and I'm in a pool of sweat with the sun raging in on me."

"I advised her when they bought this place," she said. "I just can't see living in a house where you sleep with the birds in the attic or hole up in the basement next to the rodents. Nothing but a recipe for fleas and mold. That's just my advice."

"Birds don't have fleas, Gran," I said.

"Never mind about that," she said. "Sit down and have a juice. As long as you're up you may as well help me set my hair."

Despite the fact that her girth never shrank, Granny Olga was always preparing for famine. Mornings were the time when she did all her cooking. It wasn't healthy to slave over a stove in the day. That was her advice. After cooking, she set her hair and had a sponge bath. She slept on her back on the top sheet to preserve her rollers. She'd slept twice each day before anyone else had risen. For all intents and purposes, she lived two lives for every one.

That morning, I'd stolen in on her mid-prep. The gullet of some long-necked bird was boiling next to a stick of celery on the stove. The *haluski* was just out of the oven. Granny Olga was nursing her tea and a piece of dried toast, which she gummed slowly having not yet applied herself to her dentures. There was a pot of fresh coffee for Mother.

The canister of curlers sat at the far end of the table near the window where she'd have light.

Mother came down in her skimpies.

"Lord child," Granny Olga said glimpsing Mother's form as she swung into the room, "It's not a crime to preserve the mystery some."

"It's too hot to be modest," Mother said.

"Its too hot to be most things," Granny Olga said. She laughed then. Her words were more compliment than chiding. She was still impressed with Mother's figure.

Mother poured herself a coffee and picked at the row of sticky buns set out on the counter.

"I can see you've settled in," Mother said, surveying the spread.

"As long as I'm here, I reckon I'll cook," Granny Olga said.

"Well fine," Mother said, sipping her coffee.

"It took me half an hour to find a spatula," Granny chided. "If it weren't for the heat, I'd have half a mind to reorganize this kitchen."

"I like my organization just fine," Mother said.

"Everything at arms length," Granny Olga said. "I'm just saying it would be easier is all."

"My arms are longer than yours," Mother joked sidling up to her mother's lap and sitting in it for a second. Granny Olga ran Mother's slip through her fingers.

"Put some underwear on, child," she said. "I can feel your nakedness under there."

"Why bother," Mother said. "It already stinks in here to high heaven."

They laughed then. As she got up, Granny Olga spanked Mother playfully on the bottom.

"You'll never amount to more than an idea, doll," she said. "If you don't learn how to keep a proper kitchen."

"I just like to allow you to spoil me every now and again," Mother said.

"Go on forget about it," Granny Olga said.

Mother walked toward the living room to have a smoke.

"Go outside when you're done with all that," she said to me. "If you stay inside she'll have you slaving over the stove."

"Don't act like you're needing her all of a sudden," Fender said later that afternoon. We were riding bikes on the macadam next to the garage.

"I'm not acting," I said. "She's lonely is all."

"I don't like it," he said.

"You don't like what?" I said.

"All this niceness," he said. "It's some big fake."

I was waiting on him then to say something. I wasn't sure what.

127

"It's like Father says," I said, hitting the wheel of Fender's bike with the thick plastic bat we used for swinging at the softball. "Never leave lonely alone."

I looked at Fender circling me on his bike and thought of tearing a scab off my body. For a moment I glimpsed all of Fender's future violences. The lying and looting. The time in the boys penitentiary.

"Who's good now?" I said as he pulled up next to me. I leaned into him and kissed him long and hard until I could taste his body odor where it had gathered above his lip.

I hung there in front of him. We were nervous with each other. The kiss had reduced him to something sad and soft. I thought of Grandfather, how he used to golf in the house in a pair of trousers with his big belly hanging out. Those days it was too hot for the driving range, he'd putt into a series of cups he'd lined on the carpet while he watched the game shows.

"You don't fool me," I said to Fender. "I can see you've gone soft under there."

"Sure," he said. "Isn't everyone soft under their clothes?"

"Some people," I said. "Have another layer before you get to the skin."

"What makes them worth the trouble?" he said.

"It's exciting," I said. "Difficult people. You want to discover them."

"You're not half as nice as you think," he said.

"Sure," I said. "And you're not half as afflicted."

"What?" he said.

"It means," I said. "You're down on yourself and not worth anyone's trouble."

"Oh," he said. "You believe them then, about me."

"Sure," I said. "You don't fool me."

Fender kissed me hard on the lips. "Discover that," he said.

I hadn't noticed Mother standing in the doorway. I saw her face in the crack that led into the garage from the breezeway.

I didn't say anything then. She didn't call me out any either. That night there were fish sticks for dinner. Granny Olga had slept through her alarm. The sticks were cold in places from the freezer. The coil in the toaster oven was uneven again, Mother said.

I took a few bites and lay into the tartar.

"It's not so bad," Granny Olga said. "If you chew with your mouth open. A little air cuts the smell."

We all laughed.

Mother was in her element. Meals never interested her much anyway. She only had a tongue for snacks and sweets. She was talking about all the things Father would never guess.

"Who would've guessed," she was saying. "Our Jean." She was talking about what she'd seen of Fender and I where she'd spied us through the crack in the door. Suddenly the room went silent and my ears stopped hearing.

"Which one?" Father said looking at me. A small fright was developing somewhere just behind his pupils.

"Jean's little friend," Granny Olga said. "The one with the hair."

I could tell in that moment, in the way Granny Olga pursed her lips and Father held his tongue, that this was the last of Fender I would see as I had known him, that little gutless winged boy sitting Indian in our garage as though he were about to take flight.

"You mean," Father said. "One of those orphans Ray's got working his stand."

"Yes," I said. "That's the one."

I met his eyes without blinking. His little girl was a stranger to him for the first time. I could tell it pained him.

The following day, the phone rang. Mother answered it and called Father to the kitchen. I saw the receiver where she placed it on the telephone book under the phone and Father's big hand a few seconds later as he reached for it, held it to his ear and then returned it to its cradle. Afterward, someone started pranking us in the night, calling and hanging up. I blamed it on the brothers. "Heavy breathing," Father said. "All they do is call up and pant."

"A bunch of itinerants," Granny Olga said. "What do you expect?"

For a while Fender hung out some mornings on the road in front of our house where I used to meet him. Mother said he was mocking her authority. She went out in the yard and threatened him with the police. "It's a free country," Fender said. "You don't own this road."

Birdie and I were only allowed out in the backyard. No one ever said why. No one ever said anything about Mother's absence either, or Callie or K, or no one having been at our watch all that time.

I assumed Fender stopped trying to visit about the time the phone calls stopped coming. I knew he'd broken free of me. Father had taken a ride up to their house and seen to it. "Enough is enough," he'd said during dinner one evening after getting up for the third time during our meal. "I can't live in a house where the phone is constantly off its cradle." I watched his Bronco disappear up the trailhead to the Steelheads' house. When Father came back he smoked a cigar in the living room. Mother usually didn't allow this. Father was always burning holes in his shirts. I sat on the bottom stair outside the living room and listened.

"I got up there," Father said. "And I thought I was hallucinating. I took one look at that kid and I was back at Blue Creek with my old friend Chuck Dool. The one who offed himself after the war. The kid had the same face on him. Those same wide open eyes."

"I never said he was a bad seed," Mother said. "She's just too young for all that."

"You should know," Father said.

"Should I?" she said.

"Sure," Father said. "You were young once too."

Mother laughed. I could hear her as she got up off the sofa and walked over to where Father was rocking in the chair. There was a silence as she moved into his arms. Then the sounds of his hands patting her thighs as the rocker squeaked under their weight.

"You know what else," Father said. "I get up there and find the three of them cooking dinner and watching the news."

"They had you fooled," Mother said.

"Spitting image," Father said. "How's a man to stare down his childhood friend who offed himself after the war?"

"What's the chances," Mother said.

"It's a shame too," Father said. "I never was a man to advise another man's boys."

18.

Perhaps Otto Hauser was not so oblivious to the sound of the keys or the quality of the light that day as Mother and I crowded around his kitchen and Birdie picked at his fish. At the sound of the keys in the front door, Mother looked across the table at Otto for some recognition in his face. His fingers fumbled absently with his tiepin, which he kept attached to his shirt pocket. "Mother of pearl," I could hear Mother thinking. "A bit feminine for a man his age."

"I'm home," Callie called into the kitchen.

It's hard to say, whether or not Otto had planned Callie's interruption. Maybe Callie had a sixth sense about conflict. Mother said she'd known women like her who had.

"You're just in time," Otto said. "Get in here and join us for a sandwich."

"Too late," Callie said. "I just fixed dinner. The boys were out hunting early this morning. They came home hungry for bacon and eggs."

Callie had a chest full of groceries, a bag in one arm and a bridle over the other. As she walked into the living room, she stooped over the pullout, unloading her goods on the floor and taking His Helene's face in her hands.

"You look good, Mama," Callie said kissing the old woman on the cheek. "You've still got some summer in your face."

If Callie was surprised to see us, she didn't let on. She adjusted her breast in her bra where it had fallen out of its cup as she came into the room.

"Callie," she said to Mother shaking her hand.

"Sure," Mother said. "Jean's mentioned you some."

"Has she?" Callie said smiling faintly in my direction and shaking the hair out of her face.

She sat in the chair next to Otto. Her bangs scattered across her forehead where the wind had taken them and stuck to her temples where the sweat had gathered under her helmet. The sun was out and the ride was short. She'd ridden over on her husband's 'cycle.

Looking at Callie unmoored a buzzing in the back of my throat. She wore all the places she'd been on her body. Bracelets of amber and turquoise. The holes where her ears had been pierced. The way she smelled of bing-cherry and almond. As she draped her jacket over the back of Otto's chair revealing her shoulders and her small tan frame, I was reminded of the evergreen Father carried out of the house after Christmas. If you shook the trunk too hard in the house, Father said, you'd forever be finding a needle underfoot come spring.

For his part, Otto seemed less timid in front of Mother with Callie in the room.

"That's a lovely bridal," Mother said, motioning toward the straps of leather which hung over the back of Callie's chair.

"Thanks, darlin'," Callie said, fingering the free end of one of the straps. "It's my old show bridal."

"You brought me home quite a few ribbons in that one, Kiddo," Otto said, resting his hand on the bend of her knee after she was seated and giving it a shake.

"Everyone falls into their luck sometime," Callie said.

"We surely do," Mother said smiling at Birdie and I as though we too had won her something.

"From what I remember, luck had little to do with it," Otto said.

"I heard Father say you were a champion once," Birdie chimed in.

"Did you now," Callie laughed. "Well, I suspect your father has an unusual memory then."

There was a pause. Nobody spoke. Mother stirred her coffee. "Maybe sometime," she said to Callie. "You could give me a lesson."

"Sure, baby," Callie said.

"Anyways," Mother said. "I don't see how you can control an animal in that."

"How do you mean?" Callie said leaning into the table and casting her gaze up at Mother. Her breasts hung on the place mat within her shirt. The two women met eyes. Otto covered the tuna.

Mother did a strange thing then. She took her arms up over her head as though she were applying the horse's tack to her own face. She took her thumb and her forefinger and placed them at the corners of her mouth and pulled. Her teeth were sharp and yellow in the corners from tea.

"There's no bit," she said releasing her hands.

"It's an old hackamore," Callie said. "This colt's mouth shy. The minute you put the bit between his teeth he loses his confidence. For a horse like him, it's all about how you guide him with your weight. They say it lengthens his stride and increases his stamina."

"Ain't nothing wrong with that," Otto said to Mother patting the length of Callie's thigh. "Ain't nothing wrong about that at all."

Otto got up to clear, leaning on the back of Callie's chair for balance as he reached for our plates.

"No," Mother replied. "I don't suspect there is." She shifted as though the seat had grown harder beneath her.

"Come sit with your Mother awhile," she said to me. "Make some room in my lap why don't you."

Callie got up to do the dishes. I got up to help, feeling Mother's bony parts where they cut into me.

"You don't look at people like that," Mother said quietly as I rose.

"Like what?" I said.

"The way," Mother said. "You were looking at him. The old man. It's not done at your age. It's unsightly."

Mother excused herself to the bathroom. Callie ran the water in the sink. Birdie clamored over to the counter next to her to rinse the fish off her hands. I scrubbed a little under Birdie's nails with the pad.

"His Helene used to wash mine just the same," Callie said nodding to where the water ran over Birdie's fist.

"'Don't shine your light too hard in the backs of anyone's eyes unless you want to see your own reflection,' His Helene always said."

"Mother's just testing you is all," I said.

"A woman doesn't trust her own kind," she said. "No matter how much I helped with the business, His Helene was always making sure I wasn't leaving the barn with any of her bills. When you're riding it's different. Everyone falls away from themselves just watching. They look at the horse and wonder who leads who around. All the while, all you care about is going clean and staying the course."

Otto came over with a pile of dishes. He stacked them on the drain board next to the sink pausing for a moment to lean over Callie's shoulder, pressing himself into the curve of her where she was bent over the sink.

"I'll take care of these," he said.

Callie raised her head and looked out the window sliding the long rubber gloves down her arms and hanging them over the faucet. She turned towards Otto such that the side of her body was pressed against his chest.

"I'll be out training," she said.

"Alright then," he said.

It was hard to say what they were to each other. It was even harder to say what they weren't. The way their bodies locked and moved.

"Go easy on your old man," Callie said to me from between the grip of Otto's arms where he'd rested them on the counter.

She left through the back. Otto followed her into the breezeway. They paused in front of the door. He said something that made her chuckle. The way she tossed her hair off her shoulders, you could see the tension in her neck. You could see how sad she looked. Otto closed the door behind her and stood for a minute, watching her cross the lawn toward the barn.

Otto turned and looked at me across the kitchen. He seemed not to recognize me. The afternoon light was thick and golden. It cast a warmth through the window onto the backs of the flies such that, in the uproar of their exchange, they appeared nearly glowing.

I imagined Otto fingering Callie's hairpin where it sat on his wife's dresser, turning it over in his hand and inspecting it for evidence that it too had escaped a great plummeting to the earth. "You've gone wiggly," he would tell himself.

By the time Mother came back to the table, there was swelling around her eyes. I could tell she'd cried a little in the bathroom. She often did that since her return.

"I just put on some coffee," Otto said.

"We'd better not," Mother said. "We've left Mother alone too long."

When we got home the Bottom Feeder was quiet. The lamp in the living room was off. Shadows crept around the furniture where the light had grown thin and lazy.

"I'll go down and check on her," Mother said.

Granny Olga had a machine in her heart that made her breath keep pace. It beat for her. "It's like leaning on something every now and again," Mother explained. Father said Granny Olga had the heart of a mechanic. "It'll fix itself even in the grave." In practical terms, the machine in Granny Olga's heart meant I couldn't use the microwave when she was in the kitchen.

I remember watching Father warm his dinner one night when he was late after work. Granny Olga stood in the doorway to the living room, waiting for the light in the box to go off and the carousel to stop spinning.

"It's the only time when your Grandmother visits that I can be alone with my meal," Father had said running the empty machine for another minute while he started in on his food.

Mother disappeared down the stairs to Granny Olga's room. The basement carpet was a thick brown grosgrain. Utility grade. I knew it shamed Mother to store her mother in such a space. "Basement level," Father had said. "There could be floods."

I went to my room.

"Gram's alright," Mother said a few minutes later, peeking her head in. "She's just had one of her spells. I wanted you to know. Let's all have a lie down. I can see you look comfortable."

"That's fine," I said. It seemed fine. We all seemed fine.

When I woke it was almost evening. There was a breeze coming through the screen in the window. The flies had laid off of their buzzing.

I went downstairs to check on dinner. Mother's light was on in her room. The door was ajar. I could see the glow of the lamp on her table. One of the shades Ruth had made her.

I didn't knock. It went against Mother's rules about modesty. There was no such thing as nudity between women. There was just bodies and this or that mound of flesh.

Mother was sprawled out on top of the covers in her nightdress when I came in. The long thin expanse of her legs where they emerged from the sheets looked wild.

"Oh, it's you," she said.

I hesitated to enter. There was an energy in the air I couldn't identify. Her body was prone and urgent, as though she'd been struggling with something.

"It's OK," she said. "I'm almost finished here."

I sat on the edge of the bed furthest from her body.

"Why did you come back?" I said.

137

"Oh," she said. "It was a confluence of things."

Mother was always saying that. Everything was the fault of various hatreds.

"First off," she said. "I met a man. I met exactly the kind of man I should have been attracted to but wasn't."

"Oh," I said. "Wasn't he lovely?"

"He *was* lovely," she said. "He was quite fine. Went to Harvard or something in the seventies. Now he makes films."

Mother had a strange attraction for Harvard men despite the fact that the only one she'd met was Floyd Cutler. Floyd Cutler and his young wife, Joy, had built a home two roads over on Merriam. A large single-story bungalow of Floyd's design built into the side of a hill. It had a short pitch and three walls constructed entirely of glass. The toilets required small amounts of water and the roof was designed to grow seedlings. From the outside, the house looked like a life-sized terrarium.

Joy had invited Mother and Father to one of their parties. The Cutler's had strung up a line of old bed linens on the side of the yard that faced the neighbors. Everyone had gone swimming naked in the pool that fed off the stream alongside their property.

"At first it was a bit of a shock," Mother had said after the party. "And then it was fun and then it was a bit of a shock again seeing everyone wandering around in their bare feet by the edge of the pool. The feet on those people. I remember thinking how ugly they were. The pool was just stinking with them."

"The whole thing was so damn depressing," Father had said. "The way those people got on about jazz."

"I thought you and Floyd talked about movies?" Mother had said. "Joy said you two had a chat."

"Silent films," Father had said. "He wanted to make a silent film about a woman giving birth in his pool."

"Poor thing too," Mother had said. "His wife was barren."

"I didn't know," Father had said.

"Joy told me herself," Mother had said. "One afternoon she invited me for cocktails. It was my turn on the carpool. She suggested we sun ourselves on the patio. The boys were adopted, you know. She said they were used to her going topless in the house. After a few drinks, I asked her where she had adopted them. 'They look so different from one another,' I said. She agreed. 'Oh,' she said. 'They have different fathers.' 'Don't we all,' I said."

"I think she's lonely," Father had said. "She must be lonely over there without any real neighbors. Most weekends Floyd's away at a conference. She's all alone in that house."

"How do you know how often Floyd's away or he isn't?" Mother had said.

"He told me himself," Father had said. "He pointed at the house and said, 'It's funny, Rick. I built this house but whenever I'm here I feel like I'm on vacation. And yet as soon as I leave, I want to come home again.'"

"Poor thing," Mother had said. "I always knew there was something a tad sick about that man. Handsome people too."

"You know what they say about handsome types," Father had said. "They all went to Harvard in the seventies."

"Not everyone worth hating attended Harvard in the late seventies, Rick," Mother had said.

"No," Father had said. "Everyone worth hating leaves their wife alone in a house with a glass wall."

"You think he means for people to watch her?" Mother had said.

"I don't think he means anything," Father had said. "It's all just a bunch of hot air. That's just it."

I thought of this story now as I gazed at Mother in her bed. Her head propped up on a pillow. She scratched the inside of her thigh. When she caught me looking at her, she extended her legs and pointed her toes as though to stretch.

"Oh," I said. "How did you meet this exactly perfect man?"

"I probably shouldn't say," she said.

"Probably not," I said. "Father might not see any fun in it."

"I agree with him there," she said. "It might be inappropriate."

She stared hard at me as though searching for something. I looked at her naked hand. I thought about taking it in mine. I thought about smelling her fingers. I thought they would smell like something but I didn't know what.

"Although," she said, stroking the edge of the bed. "It might be instructive."

"Sure," I said.

"He lived down the street," she started. "His father ran the bakery. He was the oldest of the three boys. All handsome too. Or at least that's how I remembered them. He was my sister's age then."

"And now?" I said.

"Oh," she said. "Now I suppose we're the same age. Maybe he's a few years older. He had some gray in his hair."

"What does he do?" I said.

"He writes films," she said. "Or he wrote one film I remember. It was based on a book of his that was optioned for a movie. The book was called *Did I Wake You Up?*"

"What a title," I said.

"Well," she said. "We were in college then."

"What was he like?" I said.

"That's the thing," she said. "He *wasn't*. We went to a few diners. He picked me up in his car. I borrowed your Grandmother's mink. But after a week, I realized he hadn't changed any since he'd written that book. He hadn't *expanded*."

"Is he married?" I said.

"No," she said. "He married young and divorced. He was in town for a few weeks visiting his parents."

"Where does he live?" I said.

"Someplace sunny. Near the beach," she said.

"Sounds *illuminating*," I said.

"It wasn't," she said.

"I'm sorry," I said.

"I figured if I couldn't feel anything for a man like that then maybe I couldn't feel for anything new," she said.

"We're not new either," I said.

"I know," she said.

Mother got up and walked over toward the mirror over the dresser. She'd hung it there so she could see the length of herself. Father had marked the wall with a ruler while I'd helped her find the correct height. The mirror was part of a set Granny Olga had given her. The wood was fine but the glass was damaged in places. When you looked in it on a cloudy day you lost pieces of yourself, as though bits of your body had drifted away. Mother turned now in front of it, examining herself from both sides.

"I may be old," she said cupping her breast in her hand for a moment, giving her chest more shape. "But I'm not blind for feeling."

She looked so young in the light.

19.

Margaret sat on the wooden stool in our kitchen the next morning as Mother brewed her tea. The two women had quickly resumed their habit.

"Friday night this town belongs to the bikers," Margaret said as I yawned and slipped into the kitchen to poke around for something to eat. "They stop for subs at *Harry's* on their way up the interstate."

Mother laughed. "If I find you sitting out Friday nights on the terrace in the center of town hitting on the musicians and widowers, I'll be disappointed," she said.

"Not at all," Margaret said. "We could use a new scene."

"Speak for yourself," Mother said. "I still have my engagements."

"Bring them along," Margaret said. "I hear there's pinball in the back."

"You're terrible," Mother said.

"Sure," Margaret said. "You depend on me for it."

"I spent my marriage preparing to be a lover," Margaret continued. "By the time I got around to applying myself, the opportunity had disappeared."

"So find a new opportunity," Mother said. "It's all in the description."

"Sure," Margaret said. "I'd try on any description which didn't involve organizing my day around when the plants in the window get thirsty and the bird feeder needs seed. Not that I mind. It's my thrill really. All that time with no one to bother me. Sometimes I find myself standing in the bathroom wondering what season it is."

"I do the same for different reasons," Mother said.

"I bet you do," Margaret said.

"It's terrible," Mother said. "This drought."

"It won't let up," Margaret said. "Lately I wake up in the night feeling like I drank a shaker of pepper."

"It must be the change," Mother said. "My mother was forever with it. I remember her sitting out on the porch one summer with a cloth around her neck. She put a fan in the window so that it blew out over the rocker where she sat. She said she needed to adjust the air in the room. One night I came home to find her asleep outside in the rocker, her nightie pulled up around her waist."

"That's a thirst of another kind altogether," Margaret laughed.

The Separatists had adjourned for the summer. Several of the women were on vacation. In lieu of their meetings, Margaret had taken to spending Sunday mornings on our portico training Mother in the ways of meditation. Together they sat cross-legged on the carpet in front of the window that looked out over our road and free associated among the throw pillows. Margaret kept a flask on her. Every now and again she doused her coffee with a liquor that smelled like anise and holly.

After a period of silence, the woman free associated while watching out the window for any cars that might pass. Mother referred to these mornings as her unloadings. To me, free association seemed akin to the acts of youthful poetics that unveiled themselves at sleepovers or the late night parties I imagined Fender and his brothers having at the butte. The more you improvised, the less committed you were to the necessity of yourself.

That morning after their session, Margaret made a motion toward the barn.

"Let's take that horse of yours out," she said.

"Sure," I said.

"Good," she said. "I've often wondered how he went."

I went upstairs to get dressed. When I came down Mother was buttoning Margaret into one of her slickers. On Margaret the slicker appeared boxy and childish. There was a jauntiness to the shape of the coat Margaret's body couldn't support. It was odd to see Mother bother over another woman. The way her hands moved over the buttons, it was as though she were caring for a child. When she was done, she smoothed Margaret's braid over her shoulder.

"There," Mother said, running her hands down the front of Margaret's coat to smooth the portions where it had wrinkled. Margaret blushed. Her eyes creased oddly around the corners. Mother's touch had a way of lighting up things to which she couldn't always respond.

"Give me time to get dressed," Margaret said, embarrassed.

The barn was quiet at that hour. Margaret had brought her old Leica. The camera hung from a leather strap, which she slung over her shoulder. As the Sheik and I entered the pasture, Margaret was bent over the water trough trying to capture an oak leaf where it had fallen onto the surface of the water.

"Tender little floater, isn't it," she said as we pulled up next to her. I let The Sheik have his head and graze a little in the yard.

"Once," I said. "I found a bird in there. Father said it had flown into the window of the barn."

"Birds do that," Margaret said. "Sometimes they loose their sense of direction and fly into the glare. Nature is brutal. It's our circumstance. Sometimes all you can do is turn your head and look the other way."

"Sure," I said.

I turned to look toward Mother. She was sitting on the fencepost near the gate. She waved when she saw me look over.

"Giddy up," she said, motioning Margaret into the saddle.

"Well," Margaret said. "Let's get a few rounds out of these oxers before the old man comes out here and starts directing us."

I cupped my hands and gave Margaret a leg up. The Sheik came to attention as she swung into the saddle hitching her shirt up around her legs.

I stood in the middle of the ring and observed how the Sheik moved under her. Margaret rode with a stiff confidence. There was a dictation to the way she posted. Her rhythm worked less in communion with the speed of the flesh beneath her and more in line with the order of her thoughts. There was a grim set to her elbow, which she kept locked close to her waist. Her eyes she trained on the horizon. She seemed hardly to rise out of the saddle as the jumps passed under her.

There was a nervous tentativeness to their whole program. Even the Sheik buried his head and bore into the jumps as though he hardly cared whether he lifted his chest or crashed into them. Afterwards he cantered off in a short, clipped stride. The only thrill was watching Margaret's skirt flare up behind her when the Sheik took a jump too high.

After a few rounds, Wilson came out of the RV and sat on the rail next to Mother to watch. He'd had a bath. His hair, a thin sweep of white, which he often wore combed over his forehead slicked close to his face, fluttered in the breeze. Wilson had developed a cough. During the day, Otto made him wear a medical mask in the house, which Wilson strapped over the thick part of his face in order not to spread his germs. His Helene's immunity was low from the transfusions.

I watched as Mother leaned close to Wilson on the rail, helping him remove the elastic of the mask from around one of his ears. "It's okay," she said, freeing him. "You can speak as much as you want out here. There so much air, whatever you have won't travel."

As The Sheik started to tire, I walked toward the far part of the pasture away from the jumps and the makeshift ring. The earth there was rocky and sloped, unsuitable for riding. I felt a pang of guilt in my stomach as I carried Margaret's camera. She'd wanted me to capture some of her lift. I'd stood close to one of the oxers and snapped a few shots as she'd cleared them. Capturing the frames gave some pause to her steady forward throttle.

The far end of the pasture was covered in milkweed. It was the season where their husks dried and the pods split. I sat down in a dense patch on the far rise of the hill. There was a feeling of disassociation watching the seed take to the air. The area was thick with flies and bees that propagated the cycle.

As Margaret circled the ring through the haze of the milkweed, I was reminded of the winter Fay Mountain had been stormed in by a nor'easter. The drifts had risen half way up the door to the house. Father had to shovel a path into the yard. There was talk of pipes freezing. After the electricity went, I'd helped Father empty the contents of the refrigerator into bags which we'd buried in the drifts in front of the house. Mother'd grilled pancakes in a skillet on top of the wood stove. Afterwards, she'd washed Birdie and me in pots of water she had warmed on the wood stove. By the time we carried the pots to the bathroom, the water had already gathered some of the chill of the house. We stood for a quick dousing. Mother took off her rings and set them on the rim of the tub so as not to scratch us. "Those will be yours," she'd said, "After I go."

We'd driven to the barn. Margaret had insisted. She needed to get home. Mother sat in the front seat with her legs stretched out over the bench toward Margaret as we drove away. "Chicken legs," Margaret teased her. Margaret drove as she did normally, one hand at midnight, one leg crushed up under her crotch. The brush at the bottom of the driveway to Otto's barn grew thick over the fence. "Blind drive," Father had warned Mother. "Be careful when you turn out."

The accident happened much the way I'd watched The Sheik leap up over the rail as Margaret had ridden him. The world slowed. Movements were jerky and halting. He'd come careening. He'd accelerated around the corner. His bike went up and over the hood. We watched through the windshield.

Mother was the first out of the Volvo. I recognized the tan of the windbreaker laying in the gutter to the side of the road. It was Wilson. "Don't move, baby," Mother said crouching down next to him. She patted the old man's hair where it folded over his forehead. Mother'd had an accident once in a barn as a youngster. Her spine had ruptured on the concrete where she'd fallen out of the loft. "Don't move her," the man who owned the barn had said to her parents. For a few weeks she'd been in a body cast. Afterwards she'd walked off.

We waited silently by Wilson's body until the ambulance came.

That night Margaret stayed with us. "He'll be alright," Mother said. "He's a good boy." Every few hours the phone rang. Callie called from the hospital with updates. "Observation," she said. "There's nothing we can do now but wait."

Margaret sat in the club chair in our living room while Father smoked his cigars. Every now and again she got up and paced the room. She had the same blank face I'd seen on Father the morning I'd found him sitting there after Mother had left for the city. "Don't stare," Mother said to me, adjusting the afghan on Margaret's shoulders.

For Margaret's sake we went through the motions. "Blind drive," Mother repeated, taking Margaret's hand as she led her up the stairs to bed later that evening. "It could've happened to any one of us."

Margaret passed the night with my parents. Mother made her a bed on the chaise that lined the far end of their room under the window.

I woke in the night to the phone ringing. Granny Olga answered it. After she hung up, she padded up the stairs in her slow heavy gait. She paused outside my parents' room before she entered to collect her breath. I reached down between my legs to feel around for something to make me feel better. Something to make me land. All I felt was the sweat from the day and the nervousness.

Sometime later I needed to pee. As I crossed the hall, I stopped in front of my parents' room. Their light was on. The door was open a crack. Margaret was standing on the deck where Father went out to do his screaming when he couldn't sleep nights. He was standing there now beside her with his back turned. Margaret was in Mother's arms. They had closed the slider so as not to wake us. Through the glass I could make out the outline of Margaret's face as she covered it with a pillow and unleashed whatever it was she was needing to say.

In that moment, I felt Wilson's presence rise up over the road. I imagined him as he had been in the barn that evening. "I'm gonna rake a girl," he'd said, dancing in the dimly lit barn. Here was the moment, I thought, when all the knowledge the world had kept from him came rushing back into his body like the third eye I'd often heard Margaret speak to Mother about.

"What's the difference between vision and *a vision*?" Margaret had said, placing her fingers on her forehead and exhaling the breath in her body until she was empty, so empty she said she felt weightless until her chest rose up again and sucked the world back in.

I had seen Wilson's face that night. His breath had steamed up the window despite the summer heat, Skeeter Davis's "The End of the World" playing on the hi-fi in the background. "Just lie back," I'd said. Or maybe Otto'd said, "Just look out the window." When Wilson had knocked, I'd looked up at him. He'd waved. "Let him watch," Otto had said.

Perhaps, I thought, this is what is meant by witness. The act of stealing something private from someone, something they otherwise would never have released into the world. As Margaret released her long, low scream, I thought I was free. I knew Wilson was no longer with us.

20.

The roads that circled the town were hilly and lush. Occasionally on the bus when school resumed, we passed one of the old farmhouses with their acres of clear land traversed by long runs of post and fence. Windmills of painted pewter spun over the barns. Animals were once again let outdoors. If you closed your eyes to a slit and looked out the window you could follow the gradations of green as the landscape shifted. A short jaunt down the road was a single story prefab, the likes of which I'd seen the tractor trailer trucks deliver down the highway. The bikers who lived there had plowed a circular drive in front of the house to park their chrome. A line of roasters littered the drive and the grove under the pine trees in front of the house. They'd hung an American flag out a window. Next was the junkyard where people brought the automobiles they'd driven to the ground. Stacks of compacted cars towered around a two-door garage constructed of plywood and strips of corrugated metal. The sign out front advertised tires and parts. A pit bull ran the length of the barbwire that lined the yard each morning as we passed.

Granny Olga had seen me off the first morning. "Here," she'd said pushing a small bag of wax paper into my hand before I'd boarded the bus. "One for each of your little friends." She was standing on the porch, her hair still wet on the curlers. Around the thin ply of her nightgown she'd wrapped the old mink Mother kept in the closet in the hall, the one she'd bought in the city.

Halfway through our route, the bus came to a halt at the end of the hill which bottomed out into K's drive. It had been some time since K had sat us. Since Mother's return, she'd become just another of that summer's passing apparitions. K descended from the steps of the salty Cape that morning just as I'd remembered her, leathered and floating. The small red door swung shut behind her. She paused mid-step in the middle of her parents' plot. A look crossed her face. She pointed toward the wooden bridge that lined the brook where the water rose when the road washed out. A large tan form lumbered across it. In the beam of the bus's headlights—the driver had been cautious in the mist—I could make out the faint glean of the animal's coat. The body resembled a bobcat in grace and build. The thin grain of its fur pulled away from the muscle. There was something noble in its stagger. Its head hung, barely able to carry it's own weight, and yet the animal continued forward despite the blood letting from the gash in its chest. From the scars and mud on its body, it looked as though it had traveled a great distance. Its torso was already weaving. Whatever had hit it had run.

As the bus came to a halt in front of K's house, the animal collapsed in the gutter to the side of the road. The engine stalled. We stared out the windshield. After a moment, the driver swung open the door and descended the stairs. Her hand caught on the stick that started the wipers. The thin plastic blades screeched across the glass. I watched as the driver stooped over the body. The cat's flanks were still heaving. A good deal of blood was gushing from its skull. She threw her jacket over its head. Before she went inside the house to place a call, the driver reascended the stairs of the bus in her shirtsleeves. Her face had paled. A blotchiness had risen on her neck. She gripped the steering wheel for a moment and peered down the aisle motioning us away from the windows. "Stay put," she said.

K stood still on the lawn. The driver climbed toward the house at a waddle, the thicks of her thighs descending toward her knees, which seemed hardly to part. A few moments after she disappeared into the house a middle aged man in an old hound's-tooth flannel came out. He went around back to fetch a shovel and a tarp.

The driver stood outside the bus smoking a cigarette as the man cleared the dog's body from road. The road was narrow. It was impossible to skirt the remains. It took both of them just to lift the carcass onto the tarp. Afterwards, the driver picked her jacket up from the road with the end of a branch and tossed it into the gully. She said a few words to the man, climbed the stairs, and started the engine. As the bus pulled away, I peered out the emergency exit. The man dragged the carcass up the hill toward K's house. He'd folded the tarp around the body, pulling it behind him like a sling.

"The Black Hills," Mother had said tracing the landmass with her finger on the old Atlas that afternoon at the butte with Birdie in her lap as the cars had swooshed by us below. The Long Walker's body, the gold of its coat still slick with sweat, was the final remnant of Wilson's leaving us. The cat had done our killing for us. All we needed was one damp strip of flesh to know that we were human. If our graces got the better of us, we could stand in that gully and someone would off us. In the meanwhile, we could start anew.

The following week Granny Olga was back to Schenectady. She was having trouble with her mechanic heart. I woke one night to find her in the kitchen making a cake for her husband, John-John. All that remained of John-John was that white Panama hat in the back of Granny Olga's Buick and his headstone in the cemetery upstate. Even his pension wasn't lively anymore. Granny Olga stood in the kitchen that night and said she couldn't find her breath. She only had a thin slip on. Beneath it, her body sagged and folded. She looked at the microwave and told me, "I'm going skating all the wrong ways."

Mother put her on the Vermonter. There was a doctor near the Canada border. "You can count on him," Mother said to Granny Olga as she boarded the train. "He's a specialist." Someone would fetch her at the other end. Maybe an aunt. Maybe her sister. Maybe a service that fetched people who got dropped off.

Granny Olga wore her fur out our front door.

That night at dinner Mother was into her wine. A big bottle of utility white. Reds, she said, reminded her of youth and all those churches with their sepulchers and their sipping cups.

Father brought out his box of White Owls and his carton of drawing pencils after dinner. He smoked a big smoking blunt in the living room and whittled away at the tip of his charcoals. He planned to lay his small-boned wife out on the L-shaped settee under the windows and draw some mercy into each of her curves.

Together, he and Mother were deep into their stash of vinyls. We were sitting in the living room, my parents still rocketing on the fibers of their imbibing, Birdie and I gutted of sleep, when the first sparks shot off the roof of the pheasant farm that sat on the Doctor's run.

It was Birdie who first noticed the flames. "Fire," she said pointing out of Mother's windows at the smoke rising over the cornfields.

"It must be a brushfire," Father said. "What with the drought."

"Should we go see?" Mother said. "Just to be sure?"

We drove over in the Honda. Birdie and I were allowed. There was no one home to watch us, Mother reasoned. What if the flame leapt? What if it found its way through the gap in the fence? We had our five acres. We had Father's land. We had all those future fir trees to drag in over the deck.

"Wait in the car," Father said to Birdie and me as we pulled off the road a short distance from the smoke.

Otto was standing in the clearing across from the fire, the lights of his Caddy trained on the pheasant coup. I hadn't seen him since that afternoon in his kitchen with Callie. He looked old, thin, nearly transparent in the darkness. Just another piece of fabric on the line the wind could blow around.

Birdie and I rolled down the windows to try to hear what the adults were saying. The air stank from the pheasants burning. I pictured the entire roost—all of the doctor's prize—flying up in one wild swoop unleashing their fetid stench. They'd escaped our Rogers and our Remingtons. "It's a shame they'll never be hunted," Otto said. "So much breeding gone to waste."

Father circled the coup once, dragging his toe behind him as though drawing an invisible line in the sand over which the fire dare not cross. Mother stood behind Otto watching the black plumes where they merged with the night. The air had a poison on it. It reminded me of the scent of ammonia after Granny Olga blanched the tub. "Amateur job," Otto said. "They opened the windows first to make sure to let in enough air for a good flame."

"That's an old crime," Father said. "Where's your evidence?"

"Multiple points of ignition," Otto said. "Next, they'll search for traces of accelerant. Looks like the work of those young bucks with the dogs."

We waited until the fire trucks came. Once they arrived, they put up their yellow tape. The men rushed in with their helmets and their coats. A thick white powder shot out of their hoses.

"Don't hustle any," Otto said to them. "It's not like there's an emergency here." He carried a cane. As he wandered around directing, he looked nearly crippled.

After they put down the flame, they turned off the sirens. The earth had a blackened hallow feel. Everything was wet. A light rain smoldered what was left of the ash.

Father took the roads slowly on the way home. We cranked down the windows and drove by all the people in their houses where the lights fell down at the end of the day. I let my arm out to catch the breeze. I thought about what it takes for a family to fall out of love with each other. Who knew how long this would keep? Our four bodies in this bucket of tin cruising the back roads of some town we only half recognized in the shadows. The rain was loud in the branches. Everyone had gone to bed except for the dogs.

On the bus home the day after the fire I found Fender, drunk and shitty. He looked tired, like some of the smut from his brother's walls had rubbed off on him. I hadn't seen him in some time. There was still that line between us. There was still the way he'd said, "Sing me something sweet. Sing me that one about San Francisco." He'd said, "You're that old man's little darling."

"Faker," I said as I passed him. "You just wanted to show up this morning so that one of us could say we heard your voice chime in when the teacher called roll. 'Fender Steelhead?' she said. 'Yes,' you said. You just wanted us to hear her call your name."

I wondered how long he'd spent washing the soot off his arms. Perhaps he didn't care. Perhaps he'd already stepped over that white line and didn't plan on coming back. He was already sitting with K, or Kat or Katherine, when I boarded. As we neared K's stop Fender began tossing packets of rubbers over the seat. The rubbers were small and red. K took one out and blew it up and the two volleyed it like a balloon.

I didn't know what a rubber was. But I knew that there was something ugly between them. I knew K would've taken Fender's hand in hers and invited him upstairs to Mother's bed. Perhaps she already had.

When I arrived home Mother was in the yard. The horses were tethered to the crossties we'd strung between the electric poles where we parked the cars.

"What about Otto?" I said.

"What about Otto?" she said.

"Nothing," I said.

"I don't like how he looks at you," she said.

"Where will we keep them?" I said.

"We'll build our own barn," she said. "In the meantime, we'll board at the farm up street. I called this morning. They've got room."

"They've always got room," I said.

We led the horses up the road toward the new barn. I thought of the night Fender and I sat on the boulder in front of the drive to the Starlings' house. I thought of the old blind guy in the golf hat and his fat wife. And too of Father walking down the road next to Otto dragging the Shetland's blanket. "I haven't stolen anything yet," Father had said to Otto.

Mother and I walked in silence. The only thing between us was the sound of the horse's hooves in the dirt of the road. "They're paving this fall," Mother said glancing down at the places where the dust had gathered around her boots. I looked up the long narrow expanse ahead of us.

Wilson's dying wasn't the last of our troubles. It turns out our doctor was a sham. As happens with the travel of news, the Ranger had misheard his story. The doctor wasn't a medic at all but rather a painter who'd attended art school in Rhode Island in the 70's. After New York had failed him, he'd witnessed the demise of his first marriage to a young prostitute and had spoiled on the city altogether. He'd met a waitress in a diner one night on his way home from scoring some hash in the park. The waitress had dropped off nursing school and was thinking of getting back to the theatre where she belonged. That night the painter convinced her she belonged to him and the countryside. He moved her out to Fay Mountain to a simpler pace of life, away from the critics and the customers, where they could stare down their disappointments in each other's company. The doctor painted seascapes and farmhouses. He sold them to local banks and hospitals. Callie had seen one hanging in the hall of the emergency room on the evening she'd gone to visit Wilson before he died, an oil painting of a single sailboat in a bay. That's all our doctor amounted to, a lousy sailboat in the death wing a second-rate hospital. This explained the pheasants and his wife's pregnancies. He was an artist and a layabout. He spent all day fucking. When he wasn't fucking he was out painting the birds.

The news of our doctor's demise was the pinnacle of the town's disappointment. We'd lain waste our hopes on his good name.

That's not the half of it.

A young farmhand had commandeered Cash's heart. The girl was also a painter and something of a talent. According to the local paper, she'd kept up in a small studio in the center of town. For several months Cash had been begging Ada for a divorce so that he could marry the girl and do right by her talent. The girl kept a stand at the flea market next to the cabinet-maker. Hers, Margaret said, was the watercolor which hung in the post. I had first glimpsed the girl out of the corner of my eye the day Father and I went to the flea market to purchase Baby. I recognized her months later by her picture in the paper. The picture ran in the Police Records section a few days after Wilson's death. The article was short. According to the report, the police had been called out to Cash's farm stand on several occasions that summer. The neighbors had heard people rowing late into the night. When the police had arrived there were holes in the plaster from where Ada had chased Cash around with the broom. The last time they'd had been summoned, Cash had been on his hands and knees cleaning Ada's preserves off the floorboards when the police arrived. Cash too had his picture in the paper. A long vertical shot of his body which made him look even lonelier than he was. His face was beaten. His hands were covered in flies.

I had seen Cash's girl working in the fields several times while biking to the farm stand to collect vegetables for dinner. She wore a large wicker bonnet such as the ones the itinerant works wore to shade their face. Father said he thought he'd seen her once sitting in the little office in back of the farm stand strumming on an old cigar-box guitar. "I'd recognize a good White Owl anywhere," Father had said.

After a while it seemed everyone in the town had once known her. Ray had seen her taking numbers from the circulars he posted outside the barbershop. She'd sold Ruth a bag of peaches for her pie. Even the old half-blind couple who lived next door claimed to have seen the girl pushing a cart at the market. Margaret swore she'd caught her in the stacks at the library taking out books. The boys in town said she'd stop by the diamond in back of the schoolyard to watch the neighborhood kids toss the baseball around.

"Where you from, girl?" they'd say.

"Kansas," she'd say.

Eventually she just said, "I've been around."

It seemed odd that no one had found her out. Cash was a quiet man, Margaret reasoned with Mother. "He provided a blank slate," she said. "It's only habit to draw when there's so much not knowing hanging around."

Afternoons alone in the box that had once housed Father's mower where Fender and I had spent so many afternoons, I used to imagine Fender and K and how we'd all once been. Fender no longer visited. The box was damp now and sagged in places from the changing of the seasons. Liden's smut had blown off the walls.

The evening of Wilson's funeral, the wind was so strong I could stand in the yard and smell the last of the season's fruits where they sat rotting down the road in their crates. Otto had waited two seasons before spreading his son out over the earth. He'd let the fall go by and with the ground now frozen, the best he could do was toss Wilson around the field and let the wind take him where it thought he should settle. Wilson never was much of a walking man. This was as far as he'd travel, I supposed.

I wasn't allowed to attend the funeral. Otto would be there and there was Mother's suspicions and the idea, too, that children should not be exposed to death. Birdie needed a sitter.

Otto's was the first car to return after the service. I was surprised to see his headlights turn the corner. After the sun set and I was sure Wilson was in the wind, I sat out on the portico watching the road waiting for my parents to return. As Otto's headlights pulled into his drive I was struck by his burden. His Helene was still hanging on, her presence both absent and livid. Every night as he climbed the stairs toward his bed, leaving her alone on the pullout in the living room, I was sure Otto prayed he'd descend to find she'd relieved him.

Callie was first out of Otto's car. She crossed in front of the headlights where he paused in front of the gate at the far end of his drive. She was wearing a suit. Something about the density of the fabric, the way it clung to her body, made her look thick around the middle. There was a bit more age on her. She was wearing a pillbox hat with a small white bird. It reminded me of something Granny Olga would've worn on the train from Schenectady. I recognized it as His Helene's. The headlights cast a radius around Calli's body illuminating the old tub in the south pasture, shining, boat-like in the yard.

It was only after Callie and Otto entered the house and the lights were down in their windows that I sat on the piano and flicked on the lamp. The piece was called "Confidence." It opened as Sterling had once described it to me, with the image of a woman on a proscenium. A long operatic flute of sighs and runs. A few measures in, there was a rest. After the rest, Sterling'd said, the piece began in earnest with a brigade of troops marching. The thing he'd said about this piece is that it contains every emotion in a single page.

Afterward, I stood at the window. For a moment I wondered if Otto was watching, and then I remembered Callie and her pillbox hat.

The TV was nothing but news. I stared absently at the images. The men were at it again in the desert. Oil drums burned in the background. I wanted to understand how far the desert was from the hole in the earth where the Starlings had installed their pool. Where was it in relation? "The Gulf" felt too abstract. Outside, the patches of grass were thick. Long and downy, as though you could sink your fist into them and your pulse would disappear.

The moon was full. In the wind, when the light caught the reeds, the field beyond the marsh looked like a river. The sheen was so thick I thought it might hold me if I stepped out the window and put my weight on it.

The screen flashed to pictures of troops in faded fatigues. "Captain Miller says anyone who isn't scared there is a fool. Is everybody scared?" Jennings said to the correspondent. I felt as though he was asking me directly.

I thought of Otto on the porch that night. How he'd taken my head in his hands and stared at my face. How he'd kept wanting to kiss like a sister those afternoons Birdie and I took to the outdoors. One evening shortly after Mother's return, before supper Birdie and I had made our way to the marsh. The box from the mower was just tall enough that, if we laid down side by side inside of it, Mother couldn't see us from the porch.

As Mother called out to us over the deck, Birdie crawled on top of me.

"Show me," she said.

Where she'd seen it I never knew, or perhaps I didn't care to remember. Perhaps she'd caught Fender and I that afternoon in the box.

What I remembered was the shortness of it, the smallness of her head in my hands, the way she'd tilted slightly to the side as we locked lips.

She'd called it the marriage kiss.

That same evening at dinner Birdie had wanted to show our parents what we'd learned.

"Show them," she'd said. "How to do it." Her hair parted across her forehead as she leaned across the table.

I thought, too, of Otto and Callie and their greed. "It's perfectly quiet here," said the correspondent on the television. In his golf jacket, he looked as though he were going on vacation, somewhere warm. "No activity whatsoever," he reported. "Looking out from the hotel where most of the foreign journalists are kept, the lights of the city are still on. You can see to the horizon. Taxi drivers are asking passengers nearly $200 to drive to the Turkish border."

"A sign of the times," Jennings said.

I pictured reams of taxis crossing a long drawn-out desert. Their thick yellow paint brocading the dry wastes of air like a fleet of canaries flown south for the winter.

The war began. Large green flares that looked not unlike the fireworks on the Fourth of July set off from the town green. "Lit up like Christmas trees," the correspondent on the ground described it.

The screen went dark. I switched to another station. "You have no idea how good it is to hear your voice on this remarkable night," I heard a young news correspondent say. "I'm going to go to the window so that our viewers can stay as much in touch with the scene as possible. I've just seen a blue flashing light down on the streets below. You can hear what I can hear, I imagine. More of that eerie silence from before the attack began."

"Is everything OK with you and the crew?" the man in the suit on the screen said.

"We're a little excited," the disembodied voice of the reporter in the Baghdad hotel laughed.

"You've had a lot of experience being under attack in Vietnam and other places," the anchor said.

I couldn't believe Mother wasn't there. I stood in the darkness of the living room and stretched toward the ceiling, trying to occupy as much of the house as I could. "Where are you?" I said aloud. "Where is anyone?"

Margaret came back with Mother and Father from the funeral. I watched the headlights turn down the drive. I heard their keys jiggle the front lock. I pictured Mother in the foyer hanging their coats. I imagined Otto sitting in the dark across the street in the armchair in the corner of his bedroom. Bent at the knee with his feet firmly planted, his legs would look like they were waiting for a kid to crawl up into his lap.

"White nights," he'd say as Callie made her way across the room towards the bed.

An old transistor would be playing in the background. He still kept the game on. Soft enough that you can't hear the calls, just the occasional roar of the crowd.

Alone in the quiet, he waits for the swing, the steady crack of the bat.

All Callie cares about is the win.

In the bed Otto's got his wait on, still shirt-tied and clammy. His hands hover, like he's searching for something bigger than what she is.

When she offers him a seat in the saddle, he says, "These days I'm more of a walking man."

She thinks what he means is, company: some beers in a dimly lit pool hall.

She thinks what he means is: I'll stick.

Backlit by the moon, she lets the evening work her body. She takes her time gearing him up. Stands at the window. Smokes a cigarette. Lets him wrap his greed around her.

"This," she says as he unzippers her dress. "Is the whole of our glory."

As I walked into the foyer, Margaret and Mother were reclined among the pillows. I wondered if Mother knew yet. I wondered if any of them did.

"I always wanted a boy for my second," I overheard Mother say from where she and Margaret sat in front of the window. The old blind man drove by in his yellow Volvo on his way home from the funeral.

"Really?" Margaret said. "What would you have done with a boy?"

"I'd have named him Samson," Mother said.

"Everything is big," Margaret said.

"My big bruiser," said Mother. "He was going to pull us out of this mess."

"Go Samson," Margaret said.

"Go Uncle Sam," Mother said.

They chuckled nervously then. That was a good one. I chuckled a little too from my place in the doorway where I had stopped to watch them.

"If you're going to eavesdrop, why don't you just join?" Mother said.

I took my place on the cushion where they'd made room. Margaret's withered breath was thick on my shoulder.

"What do you see?" Mother said nodding out the window at Otto's place across the street.

A flock of small black birds flew over Otto's barn. The wind upset the electric wire where they'd been roosting. I wanted to tell her how their bodies cut through the sky like the mouth of a scissor when it got wide, peeling back the clouds and letting loose the flap. I wanted to tell her about getting the infection out. How the bottom of a hoof turns up everything. "Sometimes it comes out natural," the vet had said. I wanted to tell her about the hole in His Helene's stomach, how her kidneys let loose their blood. "What she has doesn't jump," Otto had said. "Smell her."

I wanted to tell her about K or Kat or Katherine. All the boys she'd fucked in her bed. How I'd looked at the napkin in the basket next to the toilet that night where she'd showed it to me, where she'd pointed it out, and wondered how the blood would well up if you wrung it. Was there that much of the kill in our bleeder? I'd had dreams where I put my finger on someone's arm and pressed down a little and their skin broke open into some fetid wound. The skin wouldn't heal. The sun wouldn't let off. Even the flies were sick. They flew through the air waiting to welt you. To deliver their happiness. "It means you give someone something happy," Mother had said. She'd said, "Here's my thrill. It might be instructive."

My parents once said you could change your personality. Mother and Father were sitting at the kitchen table. They were leaning towards me in their chairs. They were trying to get their teeth into something.

It was right after Mother returned from Schenectady and her almost perfect man in the diner who made his one film. "You don't have to end up that way," they'd said. They were talking about Sterling and the factory. And then they were talking about talking and how little of it I had done lately. "Blank face," they'd said. They'd said, "Act your age. Let loose. Go crazy. There's enough time." Father'd said, "Don't end up like me." I thought he'd ended up fine. I thought he'd ended up a little silent. I thought so what if I end up a little silent too. So what if sometimes when people were talking I let my eyes wander. What if sometimes Mother wished Father's heart would leap a little more out of his chest? So what if the rest of the world came in and drowned them out. There were so many words to know. I sat there watching their lips. I wondered if they had night-lights in the back of their throats. Was there enough light in the hall at night to get up to pee? Had I turned off the faucet in the paddock where I'd let the water into the trough? If I prayed enough maybe Granny Olga's mechanic heart would give her enough kick to go skating on the reservoir again. "Untouchable combination," the neighbor had said. He'd said there was a possibility of a fourth cut that fall. Mother'd said, "No one cares whether he keeps his heels on the ground or goes flying."

Once, I'd dreamed I'd put Granny Olga in the microwave. Someone held me down on the couch and held my eyes open, made me watch her spin in that glowing box. She'd turned into one of the small Russian dolls she kept on the shelf, the one with the golden hair that looked like Birdie. I'd watched the doll as it went around on the carousel. "It looks like you," I'd said taking the doll off the shelf and putting it in Birdie's hands. "All the way from White Russia." Birdie'd fingered the doll's hair and made a little face. She'd made the same little face when the scout had stopped Mother in the mall. "Pretty mouth," he'd said, nodding at Birdie. He'd said, "She could sell cereal. She would show up well on film."

"She's got my eyes," Mother had said.

The scout had made Mother dance a little then. He'd pulled some string in her back. Maybe he'd pulled the same string that made Wilson dance that night in the barn.

"Rake her," Wilson had said.

So what if my teeth fell out. So what if that little girl at the barn was right. "Down there" she'd said, touching herself. "You'll figure it out." And when I'd gone home that night, I'd felt around a little too. "Nothing came," I'd told her. "Except this doomed little squeeze."

A patch of clouds shifted in the sky overhead. The sun cast a glare over the window. I could see the places where it was dirty. The sand from the road in front of the house kicked up and flew. Bird droppings clung to the corner of one of the panes. I imagined scraping them off with a chisel as I had scraped the back of the house that day with Birdie before we'd applied the paint. "It's all about getting on a good cover," Father had said.

"Look," I said, pointing out the window in front of Margaret. "A low glider."

A small passenger plane hovered over the power lines that lined the far side of the mountain. There was a commuter airport in the nearby industrial city where Sterling had lived. He'd taken a small six-seater to Vegas once.

The glider was moving slowly. The body of the plane was so compact it appeared toy like. At a distance it looked about the size of the model Father had brought home from the office. The model was mechanical. It was set on a long stick that you flew through the air. The wings shifted with the current. But this drone in the sky was more lyrical. It hovered so close over the wire, chugging cylinder over cylinder, like a child reeling in a kite, watching it dive and rise. The closer the plane got to the house, the more the air thinned. It hovered in the stillness searching for a current. I imagined blowing up under the body but there wasn't enough air in my lungs to keep it aloft. "Birdie," I said, watching it spin. "Keep your eye on the birdie," Father always said, his feet firmly planted on the other side of the net. "Keep your racket lifted. Don't wait for the dive."

It felt good all this letting go. I felt lighter in a way. We sat there, the three of us watching the plane train its way down the mountain and closer to home.

The landscape was silent except for the birds on the wire above the barn. I'd sat there in that same spot where I sat now with Margaret and Mother so many mornings. But this time I knew the news. It was me who held some knowledge over them. Pretty soon it would be spring. I thought of the apple trees and their big white blossoms. I envisioned K standing under the branches with all their flowers. She tossed her match. The whole head of them went up in flames. At first, the burning was bountiful. Small flecks of light bouncing off the petals where the flame leapt. After a while the smell set in.

I thought of all this as I looked out the window at Otto's barn.

"What do you see?" Margaret said.

"I see a lot of people screaming," I said.

"What are they saying?" Margaret said.

"Nothing," I said.

Acknowledgments

To these folks I am forever indebted: Thank you Sam Lipsyte and Ben Marcus for giving me the courage from the beginning. Thank you early readers: Katherine DeWitt, Caroline Dowling, Luke Goebel, Darcey Steinke, Heidi Julavitz, Rebecca Curtis, Anya Yurchyshyn, and Kristen O'Toole for your invaluable insight. Thank you to Diane Williams and NOON for publishing excerpts of the novel in progress. And to Alan Ziegler for your unwavering mentorship. Alan: you have given me two perfect mirrors on the world—your spirit and a profession, both of which I adore. To HH for showing me the way out the tunnel. To Tracy Halford for thirty-five years and counting of "discovering the woods." Thank you, Pop, for: the piano, the horses, Susan Sontag, reading me adult books as a child and cycling ahead of me on the "Free Spirit." And to Mom, for: the scope of the city, an innate sense of beauty, and always hoping the "weather was with us." Thanks, Uncle Lee, for my first Joni Mitchell cassette and showing me how to live your own vision. Thank you Ralph Woodrow DeWitt for your silent support. You never knew how far it carried me. And to Grandma for dancing to Elvis. With thanks to Kirby Kim and Giancarlo DiTrapano for making it happen. To Catherine Foulkrod for her tremendous eye. And to the MacDowell Colony for providing me peace and solitude in the final hours. And most of all to my partner, Jerome Jakubiec, without whose strength and belief I would have surrendered long ago. This is for all the spirits who long to run free.